We Keep

(The Secret They Kept

Book 3)

For information contact:
Black Cat Ink Press
https://blackcatinkpress.com/
J.S Ellis
https://www.joannewritesbooks.com
Cover Design by Getcovers
ISBN: Ebook: 978-9918-9555-2-7
Paperback: 978-9918-9555-3-4

Chapter One

It sat in the cabinet for two days, and I knew what it was. There was no stamp and no return address. The sender of this envelope had sent it directly, meaning they knew where I lived.

Six months had passed since I had received ominous roses on my doorstep. Six months had passed since I visited Henry in prison after Lucien got shot by his lover, Travis. A wispy twenty-four-year-old whose love had manifested into obsession. Lucien had this effect on people. Some people attracted an element of danger, yet you couldn't stay away from them.

It was all for the best to stay away from the striking blond model who now was a full-time photographer. That was what he told me when I spoke to him. That was a month ago.

We chatted on Facebook but didn't see each other in person. Well, I was the one who didn't want this to become a habit. If it weren't for Lucien, we would see each other regularly. I wasn't seeing anyone; I was too distrustful of people to let anyone in.

I picked up the envelope from the cabinet where I had left it. I placed it on the coffee table, but I wasn't ready yet.

I went to the kitchen and poured myself a glass of wine. I was still drinking, although not as heavily as before.

Now, I live in an apartment in Bexley. It was accommodating and nicely decorated with Ikea furniture, but who cared; it was just furniture. If I had to describe my apartment in one word, it would be safe with its white walls, beech furniture, and white sofa.

I returned to the living room with the glass of wine and placed it on the coffee table. I reached for the silver envelope and tore it open; it was what I had suspected all along. A wedding invitation. The envelope was an indication of that. The design was a kraft cardboard floral frame with initials—a vintage design, tasteful and classy.

MR AND MRS OWENS
REQUEST THE PLEASURE OF
YOUR COMPANY AT THE MARRIAGE
OF THEIR DAUGHTER
SASHA OWENS
TO
LLOYD LEE
AT BLAKES HOTEL, SOUTH KENSINGTON

ON THE 12th of MAY
AT FIVE O'CLOCK

Of course, I knew Sasha was going to get married through Facebook. I scrolled through the comments where everyone congratulated the happy couple. There was a comment from Lucien and Jan. She might have cheated on Lloyd with Jan, as Anna had confessed, but nobody aired that on social media, I thought bitterly.

So now Sasha was getting married and knew where I lived. Lucien must have told her, or he must have delivered this himself. The thought of having one of those beautiful people at my door made a chill run down my spine.

I took a sip of wine and reread the wedding invitation, not that there was much to understand to begin with; it was just like any wedding invitation. I stood carrying the small card with me and looked out the window outside. Twilight was slowly setting, and the sky had shades of blue and pink. Sasha and I met for the first time at the club where Lucien had invited me. Unfortunately, she got attacked as Anna had, and, as it turned out, Travis was the culprit behind those malicious attacks.

I couldn't say Sasha and I were friends. After Lucien was shot, I had never seen her at the hospital. She never sent me a message or anything like that, which led me to wonder why she had invited me. Did Lucien put her up to it? Jan? I thought of Jan, the most gorgeous bloke I ever laid my eyes on with his long black hair that he kept shaved on the sides, with large blue eyes and face so sculpted, so perfectly symmetrical, you would think it was carved by the gods. Jan and I had become close, not that we would share personal details about one another, but Jan hardly left Lucien's side when he was in the hospital. I had to urge him to go home and rest while I took over. I had grown to respect Jan for his loyalty and for what a good friend he was. Lucien had no one. There was Olivia and his circle of friends, but it still didn't make up for the comfort that parents offered. To feel their warmth when they walked into the room. To feel the love of a mother and the strength of a father.

He lingered in my mind, Lucien, like that portrait I refuse to hang on my wall. My phone beeped, and through the silence, it made me jump. I closed the curtain and picked up my phone from the kitchen counter. It was Lucien asking me if I was coming to Sasha's wedding.

Chapter Two

'Oh no, she didn't? Why?' Anna asked.

Three days had passed since I opened the invitation. Anna and I were in a sushi restaurant on Regent Street, where the music was playing too loud, and we were sipping on the green cocktails that Anna had ordered.

'I don't know,' I said, picking at some Nigiri with my finger.

I couldn't use chopsticks to save my life. It was rude to eat with your hands, but I didn't care; this was Anna. She wouldn't care if I licked the plate.

'It's not like you were close to her or anything,' she pointed out. 'Had you spoken to her recently?'

I shook my head. 'She didn't invite you?'

Anna pulled a face. 'Why would she?'

The scar on Anna's forehead was still visible from when she was attacked. Although the experience had been traumatic, she had got her life back on track.

'Had you spoken to Jan?' I asked.

'Not in a while. He's travelling, apparently.'

I had seen on Facebook that he was in Portugal.

'Are you still in contact with Olivia?' Anna asked.

'I speak to her occasionally, but not as I used to. I'm trying to distance myself from all of that,' I said.

Anna watched me rapidly, waiting for me to go on.

'It seems a wise thing to do. So many bad things have happened, and I want some peace,' I continued.

'I don't think you should go to the wedding. It will bring it all up again, and he will be there,' she said.

'He already sent me a text asking if I was coming.'

Anna perked up at this. 'Oh, what did you say?'

'I told him I hadn't decided yet.'

'And what did he say?'

'He didn't reply.'

'So, what has Lucien been up to?'

'I think he's seeing that girl, the redhead, Cassie.'

'So it's a girl now?' she asked and sighed. 'I can't keep up.'

Lucien was openly bisexual. They were all sexually liberated and comfortable in their own skin.

'Don't try to. If I go to this wedding,' I asked, 'will you come with me?'

I wasn't sure if it was a good idea to have Anna, Jan and Sasha together in one room. Of course, Sasha would be busy with her bridal duties, but still, it would be awkward after how things transpired between the three of them. But did it have to be awkward? We were all adults here, weren't we?

'Um… I don't know. I can, I guess. But do you really need to go?' Anna asked.

'I don't know. I'll keep you updated.'

'Fine, I'll keep the day free. Just in case.'

#

I'd always be there for Lucien even though I saw little of him, but I checked his profiles constantly to see what he was up to. He returned online three months after he got shot by Travis. Travis was now in prison, and when the jury reached the verdict, there was no victory but sadness. Only twenty-four years old, such a waste of life. Such a shame.

I scrolled Lucien's Facebook, but the last update was a week ago. He still visited his mum in prison and had reconnected with his father, although Lucien was vague about the subject. He was disappointed because he thought we would finally try to find some middle ground after what he had been through. I couldn't see how that could be achieved. His mother had killed my ex, Amanda, the woman who used to live in the house before me, and helped Henry to cover up his brother's death as a missing case, then went after me. Yes, she was locked up, but some things couldn't just be forgotten.

I went to Cassie's profile next, and she posted an intimate photo with her and Lucien. She was wearing a short dress that could be a t-shirt; she was leaning forward where he was behind her, looking like he was naked, and she was covering him with her body while he had his arm wrapped around her and her hands curled under his long pale legs. It looked like a post-coital photo to me. Taken somewhere in nature. Did I feel jealous? A little, but also indifferent towards the whole thing.

Would Cassie be at the wedding? He and Cassie didn't make their relationship "official" on their socials. Lucien had his status set as "widowed" for ages. In this day and age, you weren't official until you posted it on Facebook or Instagram, which was quite hilarious.

I went to Sasha's profile next, where she announced she had designed the wedding dress, which would make perfect sense since she was a designer. I was tempted to send her a message asking her why she invited me, but I resisted by going to Jan's profile next. He added me as a friend on Facebook when Lucien was in the hospital. He posted photos, not of himself, but of the interesting places he saw. I sighed and took a sip of wine as I noticed I had got a new email. I switched tabs and brought my email up. Olivia asked me if we could meet over dinner, and she suggested a fancy restaurant in Mayfair.

Chapter Three

She was already there when I walked into the restaurant. Olivia was dressed in a black suit and talking to the waiter. I walked over to the table, and she glanced up.

'There you are,' she said, standing, and we exchanged pecks on the cheek. 'So lovely to see you. You look divine, much more at ease.'

'I am,' I said, sitting across from her.

'I'm so glad to hear,' she said. 'Wine?'

'Please.'

She poured white wine into a glass. 'I'm pleased that everything turned out well in the end. I was so worried.'

'Worried?' I asked.

She placed the bottle of wine down on the table. 'For Lucien.'

I ran my hand over the tablecloth. 'Oh yes, we all were.'

She lifted her glass of wine. 'After all he had been through with his parents. That was the last thing he needed,' she said. 'So awful.'

'All of us were affected by it, but he had the worse end of the stick.'

'But he's happy now, is he?' I asked.

Olivia peered at me beneath her wine glass. 'That depends on your definition of happiness, Emily. Are you two speaking?'

'Yes, we occasionally do.'

She looked disappointed, as if he hadn't told her any of this. Olivia was family, after all. His mother's side even shared the same icy looks. She ran a cosmetic company where Lucien and Jan were going to model for her, but that project was scrapped after the "incident." That's what we call it now.

'That is a shame. He's so fond of you. I thought that with all that you two would'—she took a sip of wine to buy herself time—'find balance.'

'Be a couple, you mean?' I asked.

'Yes. Oh, you would make such a stunning pair,' she said. 'Your hair is different.'

The hairstylist suggested caramel highlights to my natural brown hair and cut it to shoulder length, and I nearly dropped dead when I went to pay, but the effort had been worth it.

'Yes, I did, in fact.'

'I thought there was something different about you. You look gorgeous.'

I smiled, took a sip of wine, and measured how much I would drink. I was keeping my drinking at bay, and I had

13

been good. I thought about what Olivia had said about Lucien and me and what a stunning pair we would make. All eyes would be upon us, and both boys and girls would envy me for having a man who looked like *that* in my arm. I would be branded as the lucky one. But he had moved on with someone else because I had told him I needed time, that he too needed time to find himself. I had the impression he hadn't taken this too lightly since he had been brushing me off. Did I have any idea what I was refusing? I didn't refuse him. I just wanted space. And being beautiful wasn't all that mattered. Give me a man who has a great sense of humour and could make me laugh any day over someone who would hurt just to look at him and be boring. Not that Lucien was dull, far from it, but too much had happened, and he was with Cassie now.

Lucien didn't tell me that he and Cassie had been steady for six months, but Facebook did. I took more sips of wine as I tried to picture what this relationship was like. They were living together, so there was that sense of safety that came with a relationship like that. Where one of them cooked, they argued over what TV show to watch or what restaurant to go to. I tried to picture a life with him, where we would shop for plates and cushions and bring him home to meet my parents, but I simply couldn't see it. My parents were aware of him, of course, but they didn't ask questions to risk upsetting me, which wasn't the case. He was just there and sometimes breezed into my life. Mum had branded him as far too pretty for a man. If Dad had an opinion, he didn't share it.

'It wouldn't have worked out,' I confessed to Olivia.

'How do you know?' Olivia asked.

'Well, there is the age difference. We're too different, and there's what happened.'

The image of Lucien lying in the hospital after he got shot came to me where Olivia had bought him a wooden jewellery box, which contained the two necklaces his mother had bought for him and his brother, Sylvain.

'You won't know unless you try,' Olivia said hopefully.

'Why did you bring him the necklaces?' I asked, changing the subject.

Olivia blinked at me, taken aback by the question, as she held the wine glass in her hand. 'What do you mean?'

'When I visited him at the hospital, I saw a wooden jewellery box, and inside his and Sylvain's necklaces.'

She placed the glass on the table and seemed to be annoyed by this comment. 'He told me to keep them safe and bring them for him.'

'Why?'

She scowled at me that maybe I should back off.

'It is his brother, and that necklace is his only connection to him. Amelia robbed him of everything, and so did Henry. They are lucky that he wants anything to do with them after what they did to him.'

'I'm sorry, I didn't mean—'

She lifted her hand to dismiss me. 'It's all right. Can we talk about something else? Are you seeing someone?'

'No, I'm not,' I replied.

We talked about work. I used to do a bit of marketing for her, and she paid me double than I charged. Then, one day out of the blue, after Lucien was released from the hospital, I got an email from her telling me that she was going to hire a more prominent marketing firm to run campaigns for her company. I found it cold that she did that, her of all people ending our business by email. I tried not to take it personally. I felt it had to do with Lucien not taking our friendship further.

Chapter Four

The buzzer went off as I rushed over to let Anna in and left the front door ajar. I padded back to the bedroom. There were clothes lying across the bed and shoes on the floor. It was the day of Sasha's wedding, and I was trying to figure out what to wear. I didn't want to buy a new outfit as it seemed like a waste of money, so I tried to find something I already had in my closet.

'Anyone home?' Anna shouted from the hallway.

'In the bedroom,' I replied.

High heels clacked against the floor, and Anna appeared dressed in a simple black dress with a square neckline, and her blonde hair was down and blow-dried.

'Is that what you're wearing?' I asked.

'Yes, oh, Em, can we just stay here, order a pizza, and watch Netflix instead?'

'We won't be long,' I promised.

I held out two dresses and presented them to her. One of them was the black strapless gown I wore at the house-warming party at my old house a long time ago. The other was a blue strapless gown.

'The black,' she said, checking her nails. 'The blue is too bright. Most of them would wear black, anyway.' She looked at the piles of clothes. 'Or…' She picked up a beige sand-hued knitted co-cord consisting of a sleeveless crop top and a high-waisted skirt. 'This is gorgeous. Wear this,' she advised, handing me the outfit.

'Um… the skirt is too big. I've lost weight,' I explained.

'Thank God there is going to be cake then.' She picked up a white belt. 'Hold it with this and…' She picked up a pair of pointy white high heels. 'Dress your toes with these babies.'

Still unsure of Anna's choice, I went to the bathroom and got dressed.

'You look gorgeous,' she said when I came out. 'Now come here. Let's paint your face and do your hair. I say we put your hair up in a messy updo and remove that dreadful white nail polish. It looks like Wite-Out.'

As Anna busied herself doing my hair, I thought of when I first moved to my house in Greenwich, that now was nothing but empty space, thanks to Travis. I recalled how cheery, how happy I was, and how well things were going for me. I was determined to have it back. I was slowly keeping my drinking at bay. I had been good for six months by taking the odd glass of wine here and there, nothing major.

'Do you think about it?' I asked Anna as she applied nude eyeshadow to my eyelids. 'What happened, I mean?'

'Yes,' she said. 'But I will not be a victim or let it define me. Life goes on.'

'What about the nightmares?' I asked.

She dipped the eyeshadow brush into the palette. She looked like a painter constructing a work of art.

'I have them sometimes, but… what can we do? I go to therapy once a week and take my medication and try to find some sort of contentment.'

'I just can't get over how Travis could do something like that.'

'Well, people do a lot of crazy things.'

'He attacked you, Sasha, and burned my house down, all to get some guy's attention.'

'He's paying for his crimes. There is no use dwelling on the past and asking why this and why that. We learn from it and move on.'

'I can't help it, though, and so many things still need to be addressed.'

She looked at me while applying blush to my cheeks. 'Like what?'

'Ben.'

'He was married and didn't tell you. That makes him a wanker,' she said and shut the compact with a snap. 'Now, let's go to this thing before I change my mind.'

#

A black hole grew in my stomach when the car pulled over at the kerb. We walked into the hotel I had Googled and looked at each picture, taking in its elegance and class. The wedding ceremony was going to be held in the courtyard, followed by dinner at the restaurant. There were a few guests there who I did not recognise.

I expected to see a big portrait of the happy couple, but there was none of that.

'Well, this is tasteful,' Anna said.

'Very,' I said. 'Classy.'

'I wonder who's paying for it?'

'The parents, I bet.'

The guests filed in, but neither Jan nor Lucien had made an appearance yet. I clutched my bag so hard my knuckles were turning white. I scanned the guests, the men in suits and the women in elegant dresses. Everyone had taken their seat, and our seats were at the back. I checked my phone and saw that Agnes Parker, my old neighbour, had called. I wondered what she wanted as I switched my phone to silent and placed it back in my bag.

Lucien walked past, dressed in black, fingering his hair while keeping his eyes hidden beneath his long eyelashes. Was he the best man? He stood by the altar and looked at me, and a smile curled into his lips, but it didn't quite reach his ears. I beamed at him, and he looked away.

He felt rejected, and people like Lucien didn't get a lot of those, and when they did, when people like him were used to getting what they wanted, they wouldn't know what to do with their emotions.

He had saved my life and taken a bullet for me, and I told him that he should focus on himself. To take time to heal, and then we would see. I thought it was reasonable enough. I reunited him with his father, but he still treated me with contempt. It wasn't easy for me to walk into prison to speak to the man who shouted abuse at me and tell him that his son had been shot. Henry wasn't Lucien's biological father, but he was the only father he had.

 Lucien was, as always, breathtaking. With his youthful, boyish innocence and a hint of ice and sensuality, he still managed to look angelic. By looking at him, you wouldn't know that his parents lied to him, making him think that for ten years, his half-brother had been missing but was dead, and his body was in a well in the house they used to live in at the time in Exeter.

His lover grew so intoxicated by him that he was on a path to destroy me in the process of hurting him and attacked his friend, who would walk down that aisle any minute. From a distance, you'd see someone so exquisite that you'd be enchanted by him, but when you looked closely, you saw that sadness, that bit of darkness that proved the guy had been through hell and back.

Jan walked in, smouldering with his glossy thick hair. In the distance, he gave the impression that he was uptight, a man who most likely dismissed you and poisoned your food when you weren't looking. I caught Anna rolling her eyes as he walked past. As the guests watched in awe, the two young men upstaged everyone and everything and cast their magic like warlocks. They demanded attention without even trying. Models had that power, I supposed, to make a living being beautiful. To be adored and worshipped, in this case, came at a cost.

'Would you consider going out with Jan for a drink again?' I asked.

I wanted to make a light-hearted joke that Sasha wouldn't be there to ruin it for her now that she was getting married, but I decided not to.

Anna pulled a face as if this was a ridiculous idea. 'God, no. He's gorgeous and all but not my type. Too wild and young.'

I glanced back at the altar, but Jan and Lucien weren't there. I scanned the area and saw them sitting in the front row. Lloyd walked in, followed by an older Asian couple, who were his parents, I assumed.

The groom looked handsome in a simple black suit and his long black hair tied into a ponytail. Lucien and Jan were on their feet. I looked at Anna, who was scrolling on her phone. The music announced the bride's arrival, and we all stood.

A girl I did not recognise walked in first, dressed in a purple dress and holding a bouquet of roses, and my stomach clenched. I would never look at roses the same way ever again, and I couldn't imagine what I would do if a man were to surprise me with roses without recoiling in fear.

Sasha didn't wear the traditional white. But in fact, her gown was black. Of course, I didn't expect any less from her, but she looked beautiful.

She reached the altar as Lloyd came forward. Her father said something to him, and Lloyd smiled nervously. I felt a set of eyes burning holes in me, and I turned my head to my right and noticed Cassie for the first time. I didn't see her come in. I didn't see her at all. Where did she come from? We stared at each other for a second, then she broke eye contact, and something strange yet familiar swooped into me. Dread.

Chapter Five

After the vows were exchanged, Anna and I located the bar. We didn't know anyone apart from the obvious at this wedding, and we felt awkward. We got ourselves a drink to help us relax, and people filled in quickly. My shoes were pinching my feet, and I couldn't wait to sit down at our table and take my shoes off.

'Emily.'

I turned, and Lucien stood dressed in a black damask jacket.

'Oh hey!' I said a bit too loud, and we exchanged pecks on the cheeks.

'So glad you came,' he said. 'I thought you weren't coming. Anyway, how are you? You look lovely, but you always do.'

'Thank you. You too.'

His eyes flickered to Anna, and he turned his attention to her. He held her hand as he spoke to her, asking her how she was, and Anna grew pink.

In the hospital, he told me he was done fucking around. What he meant was he would stop when I was in his life. I couldn't be the pillar that held his life in place. He was the one responsible for that, not me. And if he wanted to change his ways, he needed to do it for himself, not for someone else. His reasoning was wrong, but now he had Cassie, and they seemed to get on well together. At least, that was the display they presented to the world. In reality, it could have been different, but they had been dating only a few months, and those few months were bliss, where everything was rosy and magical until it faded. Everything faded at the end and crumbled into dust.

I sipped my champagne, feeling ignored and slightly annoyed. Why was he doing this? We were grownups here, weren't we? This guy shared the most private details about his life with me, his childhood, and the abuse he had undergone from his father and his crazy mother, as he knew mine. I had told him about Ben being married and how humiliated I was. We knew each other's secrets. We knew each other inside and out. We were what one might call best friends, but we weren't at the same time. We weren't lovers either, and I didn't know what we were.

'Hello, darling,' a deep velvety voice said behind me.

I turned, and Jan stood by the bar, gazing down at me. Neither Lucien nor Jan wore the traditional gear that people close to the bride or groom wore. While Lucien looked every inch of the gothic prince, Jan looked more like a desert prince. He wore a black jacket with embellishments and layers of jewellery that I couldn't quite understand, but he looked splendid.

'Hello, Jan,' I said.

'You look...' he trailed off, looking at me up and down, and I blushed slightly. 'Ravishing.'

'Oh, thank you,' I said.

'You're very welcome.'

I didn't know what made me look in Lucien's direction, but he was watching us, and his face was like ice. I stared at him and tried to make a face that hopefully read *what is your problem?* Jan had turned his full attention to Anna, and I saw her turn pink again. I couldn't blame her when she had two of the best-looking men in this wedding cooing over her.

Lucien stood beside me now. 'No date?'

'No.'

'Now that is a shame, Emily. Jan didn't bring a date either. Maybe you two should hook up.'

I looked at him, aghast. 'Why would you say that?'

'Don't get your panties in a twist. I'm only fucking around.'

Why were we talking about Jan? He was more than capable of finding a date, and if he chose not to bring a date to this wedding, that was his business.

'We should catch up,' I said. 'It's been a while since we had a proper chat.'

He gazed down at me, maintaining the look of ice. 'Yeah, we should.'

From the corner of my eye, I made out a petite woman with flaming red hair coming toward us. It was Cassie. I had never met her officially. Now that I saw her in person, I saw the freckles on her cheeks. Her lips were full and plump, like she had fillers. There were two piercings on each side of her lips and two on either side of her nose. Her eyes were large and green. Her jaw was defined, and her skin was milk-white. She was curvy, with an ample bosom. She was pretty in a witchy sort of way, and I tried not to have images of Lucien fondling those magnificent breasts.

'You're Emily,' she said.

'Yes,' I said.

'Cassie,' Lucien weighed in. 'My girlfriend.'

I gazed up at him. Did he have to be such a dick?

Chapter Six

Anna and I went to the table plan, and predictably we were dumped at the singles table. On the table was a woman in her forties who spoke in a hoarse voice, a chubby man with thick glasses who was sweating under his suit, a middle-aged woman, and a girl who was my age. The woman named Helen, the only name I remembered, asked me if I was from the groom's or bride's side. I said the bride, and she asked me how I knew her, then what I did for a living. When I said I was in marketing, the chubby man, as if plugged in, perked up and asked me all sorts of questions about Facebook ads.

'For God's sake,' snapped the middle-aged woman. 'Stop pestering the girl. Can't you see we are at a wedding?'

I presumed they were mother and son. The chubby man's face turned bright red, and he lowered his head. I forgot there were speeches at weddings. Lucien was the first, then Jan. Next came Sasha's father, Lloyd's father, and other guests. It seemed to go on forever.

They finished in the end, as everything did, the music began, and people gathered on the dancefloor. They didn't have a band but a DJ who blasted pop music, and I watched Sasha dance, flinging her skirt off her dress and waving her hands in the air. I smiled while watching her, feeling genuinely happy for her. After all the hardship, she pulled through and found happiness. Anna was by the bar talking to a bloke there. I tried to trace Lucien in my line of vision, but I couldn't make him out. I saw Jan talking to a beautiful woman with black hair dressed in a flowy blue dress, and he looked taken by her. Maybe he wouldn't remain dateless after all.

I opened my clutch bag and checked my phone. There were no texts or calls from anyone. I sighed, placed my phone in the bag, and took a sip of champagne. The chair beside me moved, and I thought it was Anna, but it was Lucien.

He looked me fully in the face. 'You look gorgeous tonight.'

'Thank you.'

'We are back in that place, aren't we?' he asked.

I furrowed my eyebrows. 'What place?'

He cast me a sad glance. 'Back when we stopped speaking.'

'We are talking. We're doing so now,' I pointed out.

He looked at me sharply. 'But it's different, isn't it?'

I opened my mouth to speak, but he spoke before I did.

'I thought it was best to stay away since I always seem to fuck up everything for you.'

'That is not true,' I protested.

He raised an eyebrow. 'No?'

'We have no control over what can and cannot happen.'

'I saw how you looked at me, at the hospital, like I was toxic waste.'

'Would I have come to visit you every day if I thought that?' I asked.

'Pity and affection are two different things,' he said.

I opened my mouth to protest, but someone called out to him.

'Oi!' Lucien called back. 'You owe me fifty quid!'

The other guy flipped him the bird. Lucien stood and moved, ignoring me altogether.

I glanced over at the bar, but Anna wasn't there. I looked around, and on the dancefloor, a man who was well into his seventies was dancing to "Wake Me Up Before You Go-Go" like it was the last day on earth, and he was good, giving the people who were younger than him a run for their money.

It was time to go home, but I had to find Anna. *Where did she go?*

#

Someone had lit a lot of candles, and I breathed deeply, letting the air expand my chest until I couldn't hold it anymore, concentrating on the movement alone. The night was clear, and the stars were sparkling, dotted across the sky. I thought I would find Anna outside, but she didn't seem to be there. I took out my phone from my bag and tried to call her, but it was off. *Seriously?* I thought. *Did she leave? Without telling me?* No, that was unlike her. Was she out somewhere, making out with that guy from the bar? I puffed, looking around me, not knowing what to do.

I walked back inside, but instead of going back to the hustle and bustle of the wedding, I went to the hotel bar for some uninterrupted peace. I ordered a glass of white wine from the bartender and sent a text to Anna to let her know of my current location in case she would look for me. I placed my phone on the counter as the bartender served my wine. Laughter sounded at the far end of the bar, and I glanced towards the other end. A man was blocking the view of whoever was sitting on the bar, then the suited man moved away, and Jan came to view. He was leaning by the wall, lounging about like a Persian cat. He looked pleasantly surprised to see me as if we hadn't been to the same wedding. I gave him a wave, and he stood and swaggered to the empty stool beside me.

'What are you doing by yourself?' he asked.

'I'm looking for Anna. She disappeared.'

'And you're getting drunk by yourself?' he asked.

'Not getting drunk,' I corrected him. 'I'm getting a drink while I wait for Anna to find me.'

'And then what?'

'What do you mean then what?' I chuckled. 'Then I'm going home.'

'Home? It's not even ten yet,' he exclaimed. 'There will be an after-party just down the street after the wedding.'

An after-party? Who does an after-party after a wedding? Maybe everyone did. I wasn't one to get a lot of wedding invitations, but I also dealt with a bunch that deferred from the norm.

'Do you still love him?' Jan asked.

That came out of nowhere, and I pulled a face. 'Who?'

He smiled. 'Come on now, Emily. Why don't you two just get married and get it over with?'

I burst out laughing, which made him jump a little.

'Why would you say that?' I asked.

Jan glanced down at me. 'Because you love him too much.'

How did he know? But he did. He must have seen something at the hospital.

'How can you love someone too much?' I asked.

He laughed. 'In a way, you can love someone too little.'

We fell quiet again, sipping into our drinks.

'Lloyd and Sasha,' he said. 'They got it just right, and the rest of us can only marvel at them.' He gazed at me and raised his nearly empty glass. 'To the happy couple.'

I clicked my glass with his. 'Cheers.'

We finished our drinks, and he signalled the bartender for another round. 'Did we ever have a drink, you and I, after all that happened?'

'We did.'

'Really?'

'Yes, when I ran into you in that pub.'

He narrowed his eyes at me. 'That was before, not after.'

'What difference does it make?'

'We were in and out of the hospital, making sure our mutual friend was all right. I think we deserve more than just one drink,' he pointed out.

The bartender served us our drinks, a pint and a glass of wine for me.

'You look lovely tonight. You got highlights in your hair, did you?'

I took a gulp of wine. 'I'm surprised you noticed.'

'I notice a lot of things, Emily.'

I blinked at him. Was he flirting with me? Of course he was. Jan was always the shameless flirt.

'Well, you look good. You always do,' he added.

I gaped at him.

'What? I'm not allowed to pass you a compliment?' he asked.

'I suppose you can,' I said.

I checked my phone, and Anna hadn't seen the text yet.

'Nothing yet?' he asked.

'Nope.'

'How about that after-party?'

I laughed. 'I'm not one for parties.'

He leaned closer. 'A little party never killed nobody.'

Chapter Seven

The after-party was at an underground club close to the hotel. Jan went by the bar, and I scanned the club, looking for any signs of Anna, but she didn't seem to be there. The room glowed pink, and there was a champagne tower in the middle, which probably wasn't the best idea, as someone drunk might trample over it. Pop music was playing, and the air was cold as I located the bathroom.

There were two girls standing by the mirror. One had long black hair with heavy eye make-up and was dressed in a long black silk dress. The other girl had long golden blonde hair reaching her waist, dressed in a red corset and tutu-like long skirt. They stopped talking when I walked in, and they eyed me as if I had stumbled into the wrong place.

After they turned their pretty noses in the air and walked out, I went to the mirror and inspected my face. My eyes were red, and my mascara was a little smudged under my eyes. I ripped a tissue off from one stall, cleaned the smudges off and was going to apply another coat of lipstick when I asked myself, *why? I should get my butt home and to bed.* Instead, I let a man who looked like a genie that wouldn't grant me any wishes take me to this club for a wedding after-party. I tried calling Anna again, but her phone was off.

'Damn it,' I said to the empty bathroom, where the music was vibrating through the room.

I opened the bathroom door, and I was swallowed by the music. The club had more people, but there was no sign of Lucien or the bride and groom. I looked around for Anna, but she didn't seem to be there. I went to the bar where Jan stood waiting and handed me a glass of champagne.

'Did you find her?' he asked.

'No.'

'Maybe she left,' he suggested.

'And leave me here? Alone?'

'You're not alone.'

I glanced at the glass of champagne. 'Jan, are you trying to get me drunk?'

'Now why would I do that?' he purred.

I leaned against the bar. 'I don't know, you tell me.'

I thought of the times I had seen Olivia throwing her arms around him. How each time I met her, he was there. They were so cosy that I thought they were having an affair even though she was old enough to be his grandmother, but that didn't stop anyone. According to Lucien, she was fond of Jan, as Lucien took Jan with him when he visited

Olivia behind his mother's back. So maybe there was something, and it was none of my business.

We sat by the bar, and he told me his father lived in a van for ten years before meeting his mother and getting married. They lived in a van travelling around Europe. I asked him what they did about schools, and he said they stayed in one place for the school year and moved on after the term finished. It seemed chaotic and unstable for a child not to have a home, but Jan confirmed he had a happy childhood. It made me realise then how little I knew about this man with his exotic looks and sharp facial features.

'How did you become a model?' I asked.

'At the fair. I was with my mum. This lady loved my look, introduced herself, and handed my mum her business card.'

'How old were you?'

'About sixteen. I did it here and there before doing it full-time, and now...' he trailed off.

'And now?' I asked.

'I'm old.'

I laughed at this. 'Oh please, that is ridiculous.'

If he was old in his twenties, what did that make me? He was huddled close to me, his hair brushing against my arm, which tickled, and he smelled divine. We talked about his travels, and I asked him where he was going next, but he said he was staying in London for a while. More glasses were poured, and from his travels, the conversation shifted into my eyebrows about how on point, thick, and how expressive they were, which was an odd conversation to have with someone. He described my eyebrows as furry caterpillars, which made me laugh aloud. Then we talked about when I tracked him down at the club where I needed to find Lucien after I got the roses. Jan playfully accused me of stalking him.

'You posted it on social media. Anyone could have found you,' I pointed out.

'What if I told you I wanted to be found?' he asked.

The champagne frizzed into my brain as he held my gaze. What was happening here? Giving me compliments, asking me about the last time we had a drink together? Now he was telling me he wanted to be found?

'I'm pulling your leg,' he said, reading into my frowning face.

A lot of Lady Gaga was playing, and then Poker Face came on.

'What is it with this party and Lady Gaga?' I said.

'Sasha loves her,' Jan replied.

'Oh, does she? I didn't know that.'

'There are a lot of things you don't know.'

This hung in the air as he cast me a flirtatious glance. 'Do you want to dance?'

I chuckled. 'No.'

He gave me a disappointed look, looked at his drink and then gave me a hopeful look. I ended up on the dancefloor either way, and I laughed, and for that moment, with the champagne and Lady Gaga, I felt like my old self again. The old bubbly me was emerging. I was happy. Free from worries and doubts and free from the awfulness of the past. Then Jan placed his hand on my lower back and pulled me to him, and I gasped.

Chapter Eight

The sun assaulted my eyes as I groaned into the pillow. I was lying face down on the bed. As I lifted my head, a throbbing pain banged against my skull. It came so hard and fast; I grunted. I placed my hand on my pulsating head and lifted my body to a sitting position. I let my vision adjust to the sunlight and noticed I wasn't in my apartment but in someone else's bedroom. Dread and panic morphed in. Where was I? It was a hotel room. Was I still at the hotel? Whose hotel room was this? I buried my face in my hands.

'Oh, no, no, no,' I said to nobody in particular.

I knew I shouldn't have gone to that after-party with Jan.

Jan? I looked around the room, but the bed was empty, and he didn't seem to be in the room. Where was he? Had I…? Did we…?

Oh no, no, no.

There was a ringing in my left ear, and my mouth tasted like sewage. What had I done last night?

Okay, let's regroup, I told myself. There had to be an explanation for this. I could have got too drunk, and instead of taking me home, Jan took me to a hotel room.

My dress was still on, so that was a good sign—a very good sign.

I got on my feet with difficulty, and keeping my balance was more challenging than expected. This had to be the worse hangover ever, and I had plenty of those lately, but this was another level. The room spun as I located the bathroom by balancing myself on the wall. I poured myself a glass of water, but as I lifted the glass to drink, I was hit by sudden nausea and threw up.

After letting what I had inside me out of my system, I lay my head on the toilet as exhaustion washed over me. There was sweat on my back, and my vision came and went. What was happening to me? Just how much did I have to drink? And why did I have trouble remembering a large section of the evening? This was bad.

I flashed the toilet and got up slowly as the headache pressed into my skull and lifted my dress up to my waist to pee, and that was when I realised my underwear was missing.

What the actual fuck?

Panic rose again, and I noticed my feet had dirt on them. Did I fall at some point? Had I been walking barefoot? Why couldn't I remember any of this? I heard laughter through the bathroom tiles, a voice coming and going from my head, vibrating through the room. I peed and washed my face in the sink, and that was when I saw the toothbrush and toothpaste. This room was occupied. By whom?

I exited the bathroom and searched for my bag, but I couldn't find it. What was going on? I recalled Anna disappearing. Where did she go? Where was Lucien? I sat on the bed and dived into my mental consciousness, trying to detect something. I remembered the champagne, too much of it, the music and having my arm around Jan. Because I put my arms around him, it didn't mean I had slept with him. Jan had always been playful. Then, something else came to me shouting. Someone running. Had I left the party at some point? Where did I go?

There was a knock on the door, which made me jump.

'Open up.'

It was Jan.

He banged harder against the door. 'For fuck's sake, open up!'

I stood on my wobbly feet but ended up trampling sideways. I unlocked the door, and it opened. Jan leaned against the doorframe, looking unlike his usual decorated self. His hair was wild and up. It reminded me of a deathhawk. His eyes were bloodshot, and like me, he was having difficulty balancing himself. He managed to wobble to the bed and drop on it.

'Fuck,' he said, his face buried in the pillow. 'Fuck, this is bad. This has got to be the worst hangover of my life!'

'Jan!' I called out quietly.

He probed his head up. 'Who's there?'

He didn't even see me. Was he aware I opened the door? He was even worse than I was.

'It's me, Emily.'

'Oh, you're still here.'

He looked like he was going to be sick, and, with an effort, he got up and stumbled to the bathroom. I heard him throw up, and I sat on the bed and lay there for a while. It came to me again, the laughter, the shouting, the voices, and the footsteps again. I sat up and scanned the room, looking for clues of what might have occurred in this room and possibly the missing pieces of the night before. I inspected the sheets. I had no choice and saw they were stained, and it came to me in rapid succession, making my head hurt. He and I stumbled into this room kissing, unable to keep our hands off each other.

A cry came out of me. Oh no, I didn't. But I did. I could see him sitting on the edge of the bed with me straddling him, and then he fumbled me down on the bed. I wanted to scream, but I didn't.

The bathroom door flung open, and Jan dragged himself out. I was on all fours on the bed, and he looked at me strangely.

'We had sex, didn't we?' I asked him.

He rubbed his face with his hands. 'Yes, we did.'

'How?'

'What do you mean how? You know what sex is. I don't have to explain it to you.'

For someone who was suffering from a hungover, he was quite snappy.

'I mean...' I trailed off.

'What? You don't remember?' he asked.

'It's all a bit of a blur,' I whispered.

His face paled at this. 'That makes two of us.'

He dropped onto the bed, and I searched for my underwear. Then I noticed the paper basket with a neon pink Post-it note stuck to it. My stomach clenched and unclenched as my dehydration and nausea waved into me. I pulled out the Post-it, and two tiny hearts were drawn on it. What the fuck? I peered at the basket, and inside was something nude and seamless. My underwear.

Chapter Nine

I turned to Jan; he was still lying on the bed with his forearm covering his eyes. Did he draw these hearts? He seemed like someone who would do such a thing to amuse himself. Or had someone else drawn these? Was someone else in this room? Then it came to me. Lucien? Did he know that Jan and I…? I hadn't seen him at the party. He could have left with Cassie for all I knew. Something didn't seem right, though.

'Jan?'

'Hmm…?'

'Did you draw this?'

He looked at the Post-it with disinterest and then looked at me. 'Um… maybe. I'm not sure.'

I placed the Post-it on the counter and flumped down on the armchair, burying my face with my hands.

'This is bad.'

'Look, let's order room service, and we'll talk, okay?' Jan suggested.

In the meantime, I went to the bathroom, poured a glass of water and drank. Jan came into the room and did the same, and then we stared at each other. The regret was clearly visible on my face. I didn't want him to become a regret, but that was what he was. But then again, there was always something there. Lucien saw it, too, and he teased me about it. Would he tease us now? Even Travis noticed it.

'It doesn't have to be awkward,' Jan said. 'We're adults here. We knew what we were doing.'

'Did we?' I asked doubtfully. 'Did we really?'

'I think we acted on our… impulses—'

He was interrupted by a knock on the door, and the person behind it called out room service. Jan sighed and, with an eye roll, left the bathroom.

After the room service attendant left the room, we sat around the small table by the balcony. Jan rolled a cigarette even though it was a non-smoking room and started to smoke. I drank coffee and nibbled on a croissant and felt slightly better. Maybe it was the sugar and the butter.

'Do you remember what happened?' I asked.

He glared at me. 'I remember bits and pieces.'

'Such as?'

'Us in the club.'

I remembered us in the club by the bar talking nonstop while the drinks flowed in our glasses. To him asking me to dance, me on the dancefloor, then going up to his room.

He watched me curiously now as, somehow, he could see through my thoughts.

'We both wanted it,' he said.

Somehow Travis's words came to me. *You want him, don't you, Emily? But you're too proper and wouldn't do that to Lucien. God, I'm such a bitch.*

Jan broke eye contact and smoked.

I took a sip of orange juice. 'So, you have a room here?'

'Sasha rented a room for us, yes,' he replied.

Did *us* mean for him and Lucien? Was he next door? I pictured Sasha in a suite somewhere in this hotel where she would wake up refreshed with a ring on her finger, her first day as a wife.

'Us, you mean you and Lucien?' I asked.

'Yes.'

'Do you know where he is?'

'I have no idea, but I didn't think he stayed in the room.'

'How do you know?'

'I haven't seen him around this morning.'

'That is because he could be in the room.' I slurped my coffee. 'Did we leave this room?'

'Yes.'

'Where did we go?'

He stared at the wall over my head. 'I don't remember.'

'Me neither.'

He rubbed his face with his hands.

'I have bruises on my body,' I pointed out. 'Did I fall?'

'I don't know. It's all blank after the... you know.'

Now I wanted to scream. I wanted to cry and tear my hair. I wanted to kick someone or something. I had always behaved appropriately. Yes, I got drunk here and there, but not to where I would black out. I didn't sleep with my best friend, a guy I... What was Lucien to me? Someone I was fond of despite the things that had happened. This could ruin everything. Lucien couldn't know. This would be a secret between Jan and me. How could I face him after what transpired between us? I had become that woman who kept things, but this was to protect Lucien from further pain, and he didn't need this. The guy had been through enough. This would destroy him.

I had reached a new low. I was now pathetic. I looked at the bruises on my leg. Where did they come from, these bruises? What time was it? Where was my bag?

'What time is it?' I asked.

Jan looked confused, stood, found his jacket, and checked his phone.

'A little after eight a.m.,' he said. 'How did we end up here? Where did we go?'

I shook my head. 'I don't know.'

He returned to the table and took a sip of his coffee, pondering. He placed the cup on the table, stood, and looked out with his hands on his hips. I forced my brain to remember, and something else came to me. Someone walking past me, and there was shouting, someone calling out a name. Whose name? Jan turned as if remembering something and sat across from me, looking perturbed.

'I never black out,' he said. 'Never. *Ever.*'

'There is always a first time for everything,' I said sarcastically.

He looked at me sardonically. 'I'm serious, Emily. This has never happened to me before, and I can hold my liquor.'

I was about to tell him maybe he overdid it this time, but what he said next shook me to my core.

'I think someone drugged us.'

Chapter Ten

My first reaction was laughter. It was ridiculous. Why would anyone do something like that, and why? It was simple, we drank too much champagne; we had much more than we could consume, and this was the aftermath of two confused people who had made a rushed and idiotic decision that couldn't be unfixed. Dread washed over me as though something strange had happened.

Jan stared at me, a severe expression on his face.

'You can't be serious,' I said.

'I am. How much did you have to drink?' he asked.

'I—'

'An estimate.'

'Well, I had wine at the bar, maybe two. Then during dinner, I had more wine when I saw you at the bar. That was it.'

'I didn't drink that much during the wedding, just a glass of wine here and there, some vodka. I'm trying to stay off it. I think someone spiked our drinks.'

I looked at him aghast. 'And why would anyone do that?'

He shook his head. 'I don't know.'

'And who?'

He paced around the room. 'I have no idea.'

I watched him pace the room, trying to work out something but was having a hard time piecing everything together.

'Did you see Lucien throughout the evening?' I asked.

He rubbed his jaw. 'I didn't see him at the party.'

'But Sasha and Lloyd were there, weren't they? I don't recall seeing them, or I can't remember,' I said in distress.

Jan stopped pacing and narrowed his gaze. 'Yes, of course they were there. It was their party.'

'But Lucien wasn't?'

'No.'

'That is a little odd, don't you think?' I asked.

'What? Lucien not being there?'

I stood and started to pace around the room. 'Yes, wouldn't he be at his best friend's party?'

'He was a witness at her wedding. He was there at the dinner. He wasn't obliged to come to the party, and Cassie was there.'

'What is that supposed to mean?'

He rubbed his eyes. 'It's always different when a girl is present.'

'But you guys are… liberal. You sleep with each other, for God's sake,' I snapped. 'I don't think Lucien has suddenly become uptight.'

Jan scowled at me. 'You always had an issue.'

'With what?' I argued.

'With us, with how we see things.'

I pulled a face. 'It just baffles me, that's all.'

I stood up, still feeling a bit out of it. 'What about Anna?'

He rolled a cigarette. 'What about her?'

'Did you see her at any point during the night?'

He sat on the chair. 'Nope.'

'Jan.'

He propped his feet up on the chair. 'Yes.'

'He mustn't know.'

He glanced back at me. 'Who mustn't know what?'

I walked back to the table and sat down. 'Lucien, he doesn't need to know about this. About what happened here in this room.'

He lowered his eyes and flicked the cigarette ash on the cup. 'Too late for that.'

I stared at him in horror. 'Why?'

'Most of the guests know him. There were photographers, videographers, and people taking photos. Sasha and Lloyd were there. Besides, he wouldn't care.'

'We don't know that.'

'Oh please, I've known him for longer than you have. Besides, he's with Cassie now. So why would he be arsed if we had sex or not? He's moved on, and it's not like you were a couple, right?'

'No, we weren't, but it doesn't make it right,' I reasoned.

I thought of each icy gaze, what he said and what he didn't say. The meaning behind each pause or silence. Lucien's pride had been wounded. Jan said it would be fine. Lucien wouldn't mind, but would he? Maybe the old Lucien, who was carefree and unaffected by life's hardships, wouldn't, but the new Lucien, who was icy and resentful, might. Would, in fact. What have I done? He would use this to attack me.

'Jan, please, can we just keep it between us?' I pleaded.

I hated that I had to beg for this secrecy. It was wrong. Everything about this was wrong.

'Of course, but remember, many people were at the party,' Jan reasoned.

We fell silent for a while. Then, finally, I helped myself to a croissant, and Jan stood and went to the bathroom.

He came out a few minutes later and reached for his jacket. 'Well, I guess I should go. I need to sleep off this hangover or whatever it is.'

'If you think someone spiked our drinks, shouldn't we tell someone?' I asked.

'Who?'

'I don't know… the police. We could take tests, and they would know if we were drugged or not,' I explained.

'You think they'll take this seriously? They'll just think we were sloshed.'

'We don't know that.'

'Shall I call you a cab and get you home?' he asked.

'Um… okay…have you seen my bag? It was small. My phone was in it.'

He shook his head and sighed. 'Can't say I have.'

He looked at the paper basket, and I saw his expression change. He lifted the basket, placed it on the dressing table and picked a necklace.

'How did this get here?' he asked.

'I don't know…'

He pocketed the necklace without saying a word, and I wondered if there was something he wasn't telling me. Maybe someone else came to the room, and to avoid me having another freakout, he was keeping it from me. I had to stop this, suspecting these people. They were eccentric, odd and bonkers. They weren't bad people but not the kind of people you want to be around all the time. It seemed that something had to happen when I was around this group of friends.

Jan gave me a solute gesture as he was about to place his hand on the knob, and a knock came. He opened the door, and I rose from my chair as Ben Miller and his partner, DC Alison Norris, stood before us.

Chapter Eleven

My body went stiff as Ben's eyes passed through me, and there was a slight rise of the eyebrow. Oh God, what might this look like? I was in a room with a man who was Lucien's best friend, with the bed unmade. I was still in my evening gown, and Jan was heading out. It looked like we had spent the night together. A night that was filled with holes with missing hours of our lives. No introductions needed to be made. We knew who they were; they didn't need to present their badges. What puzzled me was Ben and Alison were from the crime unit. Why were they here? Did something else happen? Why would the detectives be here if it didn't? They didn't come for us, did they? What the hell did we do last night?

'We would like to ask you both a few questions,' Alison was saying to Jan.

I couldn't see Jan's face since his back was facing me, but he might have been just as shocked. He opened the door wider without saying a word.

As Ben and Alison walked in, Ben nodded in my direction, and I looked away, feeling embarrassed. I had met Ben a few times for drinks and told him about the roses I was getting on my doorstep. We had slept together a few times. Then, out of the blue, a woman was waiting for me at my door while I was out with Olivia and told me she was his wife. She even had photographs that little shit Travis had placed on her mailbox to expose me. Never had I ever been so humiliated in my life. Ben was married and didn't tell me. He had called me a few times, then Lucien got shot, and I got distracted, but I never felt that there was anything to say to Ben. He was married. That was it.

Why were they here, though? The air was thick with tension.

'What is this about?' Jan asked.

Alison had her phone on the ready. 'You two are staying in this room?'

She looked at me, and I saw the recognition on her face. She was the one who questioned me when my house was set on fire.

'I am,' Jan replied.

'And what is she doing here, then?' Alison asked.

'She spent the night,' Jan replied.

Alison passed me a look and typed something on her phone. 'I see.'

I wanted the floor to open up and never be seen again.

'What is the issue here, detectives?' Jan asked. 'There is nothing illegal about us spending the night together.'

'There was an accident early this morning, and we are taking statements from the hotel guests,' Ben weighed in.

If any drunkenness was left in our system, we sobered up with the power of those words.

Colour drained from Jan's face. 'An accident? What sort of accident, if you don't mind me asking?

'There was a wedding here, right?' Ben asked, ignoring Jan's question.

'Yes, my friend got married,' Jan said, sounding alarmed.

'It seems there was an altercation, and Lloyd Lee fell off the balcony,' Ben explained.

I threw my hand to my mouth and gasped.

Jan's jaw hung open. 'Oh my God! Is he all right? Where's Sasha? I have to find her.'

'Please sit down and stay calm,' Alison told him.

'Stay calm?' Jan argued. 'How did this happen?'

'We'd prefer if we asked the questions,' Alison said.

Jan flumped down into the armchair, burying his face in his hands.

'Now, walk us through the events of last night,' Alison said.

This was bad. How come we had heard nothing? How could we? We were busy working out what had happened to us, which we had no memory of, and now the police wanted to know where we were and what we did. I pictured the forensics coming into this room and stripping it down to inspect each corner. Where was Lucien?

Jan and I told the detectives what we could remember. The wedding ceremony, the dinner afterwards, running into Jan, going to the after-party, and ending up in his hotel room. I didn't mention the other distorted memories: the shouting, the bruises on my leg, that someone might have spiked our drink. Where was Anna?

'Was there alcohol?' Ben asked.

'Yes,' Jan replied.

'So, you two went to the after-party?' Alison asked.

'Yes,' Jan said.

Alison typed on her phone. 'How long did you stay there? An estimate.'

'Not sure. About two hours,' Jan said.

'And where did you go afterwards?' Alison asked.

'We came here,' Jan said.

'And you spent the night together?' Alison asked.

'Yes,' Jan confirmed.

'Where is Sasha?' I asked.

'She's been taken to the station,' Alison remarked.

'To the… why? Is she under arrest?' Jan asked.

'We just need to take a statement. She's in shock,' Ben said.

'So, Lloyd is…' Jan trailed off, unable to finish.

'Deceased, yes,' Alison said.

There was an air of shock as we both took this in. Lloyd was dead. Sasha had been a wife for less than twenty-four hours, and now she was a widow. *Poor girl*, I thought. What happened to us seemed so small and petty compared to what she was going through. To be grieving and have the police asking you difficult questions. What happened between her and Lloyd that led him to fall off the balcony to his death? What on earth would they argue about after their wedding night? Maybe he took the wrong step and fell, but why were they asking us all those questions if it was an accident? Where we'd been? Who we saw? How much we had to drink? I had been around the police enough to know why. Because it wasn't an accident. They wouldn't tell us, so they wouldn't alarm us, but they must have suspected at least that Lloyd falling off the balcony was no accident at all. That someone pushed him. It was murder.

'Did any of you see Lucien Jones?' Alison asked.

My body went cold as a new kind of terror surged into me. Why were the police asking us where he was? Where was he? What if something happened to him too?

'I saw him at the wedding,' Jan replied.

'But not at the after-party?' Alison asked.

'No,' Jan said.

Alison turned to me. 'What about you? Did you see him?'

'At the wedding. May I ask why?' I asked.

'We are looking for him. According to Cassie Abbot, he left the hotel around midnight and hasn't been seen since,' Ben said.

Chapter Twelve

What did they mean he hasn't been seen since? Was Lucien missing? Not missing, that wouldn't be right. If he left the hotel at midnight, wasn't he at the apartment? The police must have looked for him there. It was the first place they would look, and if they were asking us, that meant they didn't know where he was. Did he flee? Where? Why? Was he part of the altercation? Now I wished I had taken Anna's suggestion, stayed at home, ordered a pizza and binged in front of Netflix, and all of this would have been avoided. Where did he go?

Ben and Alison pocketed their phones and thanked us for our time before they left. Ben cast a backward glance at me before shutting the door.

Jan and I looked at each other.

'What the fuck?' he said.

'Jan, what the fuck happened last night?' I asked.

'I don't know.'

He stood. 'We were drunk.'

'Where the hell is Lucien?'

'I have no idea,' he said.

He took out his phone.

'Did he text you?' I asked.

'No,' Jan said, composing a text, then pocketed the phone. 'I'm going to find out what is going on.'

I looked around the room as the panic resurfaced. 'Why can't I find my bag? Where is it?'

'Calm down, Emily, we will find it after I find out what the hell is going on,' Jan said.

'I'm coming with you,' I said. 'Maybe I will find Anna.'

He sighed dramatically. 'Fine.'

#

As we stood in the corridor, I saw a man in a suit standing two doors away, and I heard the flashing of cameras and voices. A uniformed policewoman saw us and told us to go into our rooms. There was nothing to see here. There was plenty to see, but we obeyed and went back inside the stuffy suite. Were they going to keep us there? Jan shut the door, and a phone rang. Jan cast me a confusing look, and I tried to determine where the ringing was coming from. I knelt on all fours, looking under the bed. My bag was in the middle of the floor, but I couldn't reach it.

'My bag is under the bed. I can't reach it,' I said.

The phone stopped ringing.

Jan went down on his knees, and after a few attempts, he got my bag. He stood and sat on the armchair, scrolling on his phone. I opened my clutched bag and took out my phone. My phone could give us an insight into what had happened. There were three missed calls, two texts, and two Facebook messages. I checked the missed calls first. The recent call was from Mrs Parker. What did she want? Why did she keep calling me? Had she seen something? The other missed calls were from Olivia and Anna. Next, I went to text messages. They were both from Anna sent last night.

The first one was sent at around midnight.

Emily! Where are you?

The second text was sent half an hour later.

It seems like you've got busy or something. I'm going home. Speak soon x.

I called Anna, but she didn't pick up. I didn't have the energy to speak to Mrs Parker, not now at least, and I couldn't deal with a nosy neighbour right now.

Then it came to me. Maybe Lucien went to Olivia. That was why the police couldn't find him. Why would he go there unless something happened last night that upset him, and he didn't want to be found by anyone? But if Mrs Parker saw him going into Olivia's house, he would be found in no time. Or did Lloyd fall off the balcony and make it to the news? Unless she saw him with Sasha when his parents lived in the house with the yellow door. I was driving myself crazy with questions.

Olivia picked up on the third ring.

'Emily?'

'Olivia, hi, sorry for not taking your call. Is everything all right?'

'The police were here. They are looking for Lucien. Wasn't he at the wedding?'

'You didn't speak to him.'

'No. What happened? The police wouldn't tell me anything. Were you at the wedding?'

Jan was looking at me now.

'Yes, I was,' I said.

'What happened?' she demanded.

Jan was now in front of me and extended his jewelled hand. I handed him my phone, and he turned away from me. I didn't want to imagine Olivia's confusion about Jan being with me. The fewer people who knew we were together, the better.

'I will. Bye,' he said and handed me my phone.

'What did she say?' I asked.

'The police are looking for Lucien,' he said.

'Any idea where he might be?'

'No.'

'What about Cassie?'

'I texted her, but she hasn't replied yet.'

I went to my phone to see if something was incriminating on there, but it didn't look like I had taken any photos. What about social media? What was out there? What if I got tagged?

'Jan.'

'Yes, Emily?'

'Did you take any pictures with your phone?' I asked.

It seemed like the thought hadn't occurred to him as he went to his phone and tapped on it.

'No. Nothing,' he informed.

'What do you think happened between Sasha and Lloyd?'

'I don't know… it's like they got into an argument of some sort, and he might have slipped and fallen. That's what I think.'

'Why are the police investigating then if it was an accident?'

'The police are always involved in accidents.' He looked me up and down. 'What are you suggesting, Emily? That she pushed—' He paused, and there was a look of horror on his face.

'What? What's wrong?' I asked, alarmed.

'I think I saw someone,' he said.

I went to him. 'Who did you see?'

'On my way here, as I was walking to the corridor, I think I saw someone going inside Lloyd's room.'

'Did you see who it was?'

I shook his head. 'It's all muffled, but he opened the door, which meant he knew who it was.'

'Was it Sasha?'

'No, definitely not her. The hair would have been a dead giveaway.'

I noted that with her purple hair, Sasha would be spotted from miles away.

'Maybe we should inform the police.'

He looked up. 'I'm not sure what I saw… I could be wrong. It could be a member of staff. You know, room service.'

'Was it a man or a woman?' I asked.

He looked doubtful. 'I'm not sure.'

Chapter Thirteen

When I arrived at the apartment, it was nearly lunchtime. My evening gown looked tattered and needed a dry clean. I was completely sober by then, just slightly drowsy and disorientated.

I stripped off my dress and underwear and threw them in the washing basket to deal with later. I walked to the window and moved the curtains an inch; the sky was blue, and people were passing by with their shopping bags to prepare their Saturday meals with their families while I would spend it alone. I needed to be alone and get my bearings on what happened that night and how Lloyd had died. I went to the bathroom, filled the bath with warm water, and poured bath salts and oils. While I waited, I inspected the purple bruises on my calf and knees.

I lay in the bath and noticed a bruise on my nipple. It took a while to realise it wasn't a bruise but a love bite. I stared at the tiles, my eyes wide with shock. Never had I thought I would do something like this. Something that was so out of character.

I rubbed my face with my hands. How could I allow myself to behave so foolishly? I should have acted like this in my twenties, not now in my thirties. What was wrong with me? Had Jan even considered using protection? We were so plastered and off our faces that it didn't even occur to either of us. I didn't see any condom wrappers in the room, and I wasn't on the pill.

A new sense of alarm hit me like a brick.

'Great,' I said.

I pictured all the scenarios in my head: me pregnant, Jan refusing to believe that the child was his and Lucien feeling betrayed. What a shitty thing to do, and the thing was that Jan didn't feel any sense of guilt. Would Lucien mind? Well, Sasha slept with both of them, and they remained friends, but I wasn't Sasha. Comparing myself to her was useless. She was a young, beautiful woman who shared the same beliefs. I found their lifestyle too colourful compared to my pedestrian life. Now Lucien was missing. Where could he be? Did he go to Exeter? But that house was sold.

I thought of places he'd told me about, but thinking about it, Lucien hardly mentioned anything that sparked an interest. Some festivals popped up every now and then. Had he gone to a festival? Alone? Without telling anyone? Why would he be secretive about it if he did go to a festival?

After my bath, I put on my pyjamas and took my laptop to bed. I checked my phone, and there was yet nothing from Anna. I tried calling her again, but there was no answer. Where was she? Did I need to call her dad? But I didn't want to worry him. I'd give it more time. I opened my laptop and searched to see if there was any mention of the accident or murder. There was nothing yet, and some crimes barely made it to the news. I thought of what Jan had said, that we might have been drugged, and he might have seen someone go into Lloyd's room. Was it room service, or was it someone else? Someone he knew?

I closed the tab, went to Facebook, and checked Lucien's profile. He was tagged on many photos, selfies mostly of happy faces I didn't know and wouldn't know. A photo went past, and I went back to it. A professional photographer had taken this photo. Lucien with two girls, one blonde and one with raven hair. The dark one dressed in a silky black dress that looked like a nightie, the blonde in a red corset and tutu-like long skirt. The girls from the bathroom. I remembered how they stopped talking when I walked in. Did they know me? How? I had never seen them before in my life. Now, everyone was a suspect in my eyes. I tried to see if the girls were tagged, but only Lucien was.

I went to Jan's profile; he was tagged in many photos. I inspected each one, but I didn't appear to be in his company, which was a relief. Why was I bothering to keep this a secret? The police knew we had slept together, and the news would travel back to Lucien. Where was he? I picked up my phone and tried calling him, but his phone was off.

I flipped to Jan's photos, and the two girls appeared again; they weren't tagged either since the photographer had taken them. I looked for Sasha's profile next. She was the one that was tagged the most, and I flipped through the photos, and the girls were there too. Not tagged. They posed individually with Sasha, and she seemed close to them. Who were those girls? Why did I feel like they knew something? I returned to Jan's profile, but his friend list wasn't visible. Neither was Lucien's or Sasha's. They were being more cautious now, given everything that had happened. And that left me with a dead end.

#

I was having a nightmare where I was being chased by Ed. His skin was tattering, and bugs were coming out of his mouth when my phone went off. It had gone dark out, and the rain was hitting the windows. I fumbled for my phone and saw it was Anna.

'Emily!' Anna hissed into my ear. 'What the fuck? I was so worried. Where were you? I ran into an old friend, and we had a drink, then I went to the bathroom, and I couldn't find you anywhere.'

'I looked for you in the bathroom. I didn't see you,' I said.

'I also went outside, thinking you were there, but you disappeared. Why didn't you call?'

'I texted you. You didn't reply. Gosh, it was a strange night and—'

'Are you at your place?'

'Yes.'

'I'm coming over.'

'Oh.' I looked at the time. It was only 8:30 p.m. 'Okay.'

#

'I brought sushi,' Anna announced when she arrived at my apartment thirty minutes later.

'Thank you,' I said, opening the door wider for her to come in.

'Oh, and I found this,' she said, handing me a brown envelope. 'It was on the floor. It must have dropped from the letter box.'

'Cheers,' I said.

I took the envelope from her and placed it on the coffee table along with the sushi.

'How are you? You look tired,' she said.

'I am.'

'Long night?'

'You can say that again.'

She blinked at me. 'Are you all right?'

I rubbed my forehead and went to the kitchen to make the Band-Aid for all my problems. Tea.

I put the kettle on and opened the cupboards. 'Did you hear what happened at the hotel this morning?'

She leaned against the doorframe. 'Can't say I have.'

I placed the mugs on the counter and turned to her. 'Lloyd fell to his death.'

Her jaw dropped. 'Oh, my God, that's horrible. Sasha must be devastated. Poor girl.'

'The strange thing is the police came to ask questions. Well, Ben did.'

Her eyes went wide. 'Ben?'

The kettle boiled, and I placed two tea bags in the mugs and poured hot water. 'Yes.'

She blinked rapidly. 'But he's in the crime unit. Do they think it's murder?'

I nodded as I opened the fridge and took out the milk.

'Oh my God.'

I handed her a mug of tea and walked to the living room.

'I should have listened to you,' I said. 'I shouldn't have gone to that wedding. Each time I'm in a room with those people, something awful happens, and I end up getting sucked back in.'

'But this is not your fault. You couldn't have known this was going to happen. How could you?'

'I know, but...' I trailed off.

I wasn't going to tell her about Jan or about the blackout.

She rubbed my knee. 'Oh, Em, don't blame yourself. Where did you go?'

'To the after-party.'

She stared at me. 'There was an after-party?'

'Yes, you didn't know?'

'No, nobody said anything to me, not that I would have gone. You went?'

I took a sip of tea. 'Yes.'

'How was it?'

'Like any other party.'

'What about Lucien?' she asked.

'What about him?' I asked.

'How did he take all of this? He was friends with Lloyd. He must be devastated.'

'Lucien is missing.'

'Missing? How come?'

'I don't know... he left the wedding around midnight and hasn't been seen since.'

'Jesus, all of this happened last night?' she asked in disbelief.

'Yep.'

'Have you tried calling him?'

'I did. He's not picking up, and—'

My phone beeped with a text message making me stop mid-sentence, and the circle of Jan's profile appeared. I pocketed my phone before Anna saw it and questioned why Jan was texting me, although she knew we kept in touch when Lucien was in the hospital.

After Anna left, I placed the remaining sushi in the fridge for lunch tomorrow and walked to the living room to clear up. I picked up the envelope and tore it open. Something dropped on the floor by my feet. I frowned as I realised it was a condom. *What on Earth?* I picked it up, placed it on the coffee table, and folded the letter.

Hope you had fun at the wedding.

The note was typed, and the sender was unknown. Who had sent this? Lucien? Did he send this? But why would he send me an unused condom and an anonymous note? No, this was someone else.

Hope you had fun at the wedding.

Then I understood what it meant. The condom and the note. Someone knew about Jan and me.

Chapter Fourteen

Olivia had requested an audience at her house. It was the first time I was going to go inside that house with its yellow door since Lucien's parents had been arrested. Shivers went down my spine when I saw what was left of my house, which was nothing but an empty space. My beautiful home had been touched by such ugliness and secrets that I had no choice but to move out.

I hurried my pace to avoid being seen, especially by Mrs Parker, who I hadn't yet called back. I entered the short walkway to Olivia's house, rang the bell and stared at the welcome mat while waiting.

'Emily,' Olivia said, opening the door wider. 'Come in.'

She held the door for me, and before shutting the door, she checked the area.

'A habit,' she said, gesturing for me to walk through.

I almost stopped dead in my tracks as I approached the living room. It was like I had stepped into a different house. Gone was the furniture dating from the 70s or the 80s, and in came the shabby chic décor. I expected a woman as elegant as Olivia to go for contemporary or minimalistic décor, but there you have it.

'I love what you did to the place,' I said.

Olivia fingered her pearl necklace and looked at the décor as if seeing it for the first time.

'Yes, it was long overdue. Amelia had no taste, not that she was in the right state of mind for it, and Henry, well, he's a simple man.'

Maybe that was why Amelia needed something to keep her occupied besides baking cakes all day. It could have been some form of therapy. *Maybe I should take up something like gardening or take cooking lessons.*

Olivia gestured to the kitchen. It was green with a counter in the middle, and the air smelled of toast and bacon.

'Husband at work?' I asked.

'Yes, he's at the clinic. It's amazing how many beauty procedures people need,' she said.

Her husband was a cosmetic surgeon, hence why she looked so amazing. I never had the pleasure of meeting Mr Mitchell in the flesh. Olivia went to the stove and put the kettle on. My phone pinged with a Facebook message, and the circle of Jan's profile picture appeared on my screen. I hadn't replied to his messages yet where he had asked me to meet up. I was too distracted by the mysterious letter and forgot to reply.

I sighed as I read the text, Jan asking me this time if I was still alive. I placed the phone on the table and sighed once more. I found Jan utterly fascinating; now he was becoming a regret and a secret.

My phone pinged once more. It was him again, now telling me to come to his apartment at 7 p.m. I stared at the text with my mouth gaped open. He wasn't asking, but ordering. Why at his apartment? Why not at the pub down the street? I had been stepping into dangerous territory long enough. It was like we were having an affair.

Olivia placed a teacup in front of me while I chewed on my bottom lip as I placed the phone on the table. The chat was open, and I accidentally hit the thumbs-up emoji. I slapped my hand on my forehead as the circle of Jan's picture dropped, showing he had seen the message.

Fuck.

'Oh my,' Olivia said. 'You look flustered.'

'Oh, I…' I stammered and closed the app.

'Emily,' she said, all serious now.

It made me feel like I had been summoned to the headmistress's office.

'I heard about what happened at the wedding,' she announced.

Lots of things happened at that wedding. Which part had she heard?

'You mean about the groom?' I asked.

'Yes, such tragedy, poor girl. Another policeman came here asking questions.'

'They came here twice?'

'Yes, this time it was Miller, I believe he said his surname was. Well dressed. Handsome,' she pointed out.

Ben was here asking Olivia questions? It was his job to ask questions; that was how he caught his killer. Having Ben back in my orbit felt weird, especially since I had been avoiding him for months.

'Has Lucien been in touch?' I asked.

'No, I'm worried about him. Hence why I asked you here.'

'I don't know where he is.'

'Neither does Jan.'

His name loomed over her cosy kitchen.

'You were together the night after the wedding?' she asked.

No point in lying.

I felt the heat rush into my face. 'Yes.'

'No need to blush, dear. I know Jan can have a strange effect on people. He's just…' She paused, looking for the right word. 'Lovely,' Olivia said. 'When he walks into the room, it blooms with his loveliness.'

The image of us together flashed before me, and I took a sip of my tea to dismiss it. Yes, he was lovely and bold.

'What about Lucien's girlfriend? Have you got a hold of her?' I asked.

She looked at me with utter surprise. 'Girlfriend? What girlfriend? Since when has Lucien had a girlfriend?'

'Um…' I stammered.

Didn't he tell her about Cassie? Had I overstepped? Was I supposed to keep my mouth shut?

'Since…err… on Facebook… they look quite steady. They're living together,' I said. 'And he introduced her to me as his girlfriend.'

'Well, I had no idea.'

Strange. Lucien was close to Olivia. This was the guy who kept his visits to her from his mother, and he wouldn't tell her he was living with a woman. Where did he tell her he was living then?

'You don't know?' I asked.

'I know he moved out from Jan's place, a terrible idea if you ask me,' Olivia confessed. 'He said he was living with someone but didn't reveal if it was a man or a woman. So, he's living with a girl, then?'

I blinked at her. 'Yes. Don't you find it strange he didn't tell you any of this?'

'Oh, Lucien became secretive after he was shot. I never quite know what's on his mind. He has been through a lot, so obviously he's going to change. But it feels like it was overnight. He's become detached, distant and cold. More reserved. Angry. Didn't you notice?'

'Well, he seems different.'

'I think it has to do with those visits to prison. He should stop them. They're not good for him. He doesn't need all of that negativity in his life, not after what he has been through. You're the one who reunited Lucien with Henry, correct?'

'Yes, I thought it was the right thing to do given what happened, don't you agree?'

She took a sip of tea, saying nothing to this. It was obvious she disagreed and that I might have stuck my nose where it didn't belong. Maybe I should have left it alone.

'You never met her, Cassie?' I asked.

'No,' said Olivia. 'I didn't know she existed until now.'

'Oh.'

She narrowed her eyes at me. 'I don't think it's that serious, is it?'

If he was living with her, it had to be serious. It was as serious as one could get in a relationship, but I had to remember that I was dealing with a group of people who didn't do things the conventional way. Maybe they had some sort of agreement he'd live with her, and from time to time, they shared a bed.

'He's a gorgeous man with needs,' Olivia added. 'I don't think he would allow someone in that easily after all that's happened to him.'

I disagreed with her. Not everyone who has been through an unpleasant experience shuts people out. I haven't, to some extent. I could admit a relationship was the last thing on my mind.

'I thought he'd be in touch with you since he loves you,' Olivia said.

'He hasn't. I'll tell you if he gets in touch, and can you please let me know if he calls?'

'Of course.'

'What did the detective tell you?' I asked.

'That he was looking for Lucien to ask him a few questions. He told me what had happened and that Lloyd's death wasn't accidental. They believe it was murder.'

'What about Sasha?'

'You know how it is. It's always the spouse who gets the blame.'

'Is she under arrest?'

'I don't know, dear.'

'That is… how did it turn out this way? Getting married is supposed to be the happiest day of your life.'

'Oh, please,' Olivia said.

I blinked at her.

'You're so sentimental, Emily. You think getting married to a man is the happiest day of a woman's life?'

'Why wouldn't it be if he's the love of her life?' I argued.

'Rubbish,' she grumbled.

'Weren't you happy when you got married?'

'Of course I was happy, but the happiest day of my life was when I opened my company.'

'To each their own, I guess,' I said.

Chapter Fifteen

When I left Olivia's house, I glanced again at where my house once used to be. A house I loved, to a house I hated, to the one I couldn't sell. Now it was demolished by the fire, and I was left with the memories of it. How happy I was when I moved there, and I never took a single photo of that house.

'Emily!'

My insides turned to liquid.

'Emily, dear!'

I hadn't returned her calls, and Agnes had seen me. I fixed a toothy grin that made my jaw hurt and turned.

'Agnes, hi! So wonderful to see you! How are you?'

Too cheery, I thought.

'I called you. I was worried when you hadn't returned any of my calls.'

'I was... busy. You know how it is. It completely slipped my mind. You look well.'

'You look tired,' she pointed out. 'Aren't you sleeping? You young people these days, all you want to do is work.'

I smiled through gritted teeth.

'A policeman was here,' she said.

Was Ben asking questions to Agnes Parker too? Of course he was. I bet the neighbours pointed him to her door. She was the one who saw everything.

'I see. What did he say?'

'Why don't you come in for a cuppa?' she suggested.

I needed to go back home and catch up on work, but if I accepted her offer, I could catch up on the scoop. Lucien and I had entertained this woman long enough, but I had to ask her if she had seen him. If there was someone who would know, it was her.

'Love to,' I said.

The curtain of Olivia's house moved, and she cast me a sympathetic glance before quickly closing it again. I followed Agnes to the house, and she made me sit in her spotless living room that smelt of floor detergent and floral air freshener while she skipped to the kitchen.

'How is the new apartment?' she asked.

'Delightful,' I said.

'Better than a house?'

'Yes, easier to clean,' I said.

'Oh yes, much more efficient. I get a cleaning lady twice a week. I just don't have the energy anymore.'

Agnes appeared with a tray of teacups and a pot of tea. I attempted to help her, but I was dismissed. She handed me a cup of tea and offered me a shortbread. I took one and munched on it slowly.

'So, the handsome detective,' she said.

I was glad she was getting to the point.

'Yes,' I said.

'Is Lucien all right?' she asked.

'Why wouldn't he be?' I asked.

'Well, you would know,' she said. 'Giving your history with the lad.'

This hung in the air.

'We talk, but it's not like he tells me everything,' I said.

'How strange. Aren't you in a relationship with him?'

Where did she get that information from? Was that what she told Ben? That I was in a relationship with Lucien?

'I'm not,' I said, not that I needed to justify myself to this woman.

'Oh, I thought you were,' she said.

What gave her that idea? It's not like it was any of her business.

'What did the detective ask?' I asked, keeping her on the subject.

'If I knew where Lucien was, if I had seen him and how long I've known him.'

'And what did you tell him?'

She poured sugar into her tea. 'That I knew him since he moved with his parents, and I had seen him on Friday night.'

I perked up at this. 'You saw him on Friday night?'

She took a sip of tea. 'Well, early Saturday morning.'

'Where?' I asked.

'I went to use the bathroom and saw him standing by Olivia's house.'

I looked at her, confused. 'You mean he just stood there and didn't go in?'

'Yes. It was most bizarre. He was smartly dressed, so I knew he'd been at a wedding.'

Did Olivia know about this? If he went in, I don't think she was aware. What was he doing just standing there by the house? *Wait… did she say a wedding?* How did she know about that?

'How did you know he was at a wedding?'

'The detective told me, of course, and told me what happened.'

'I see,' I said. 'Did you see what he did afterwards?'

'Yes, he got into a car and drove off.'

I stared at her. 'He drove?'

'Yes.'

But Lucien didn't own a car.

'Are you sure he was the one driving?'

Agnes looked down at the carpet, unsure now. 'Yes, it was definitely him driving. He got in from the driver's seat.'

'But Lucien doesn't own a car,' I said.

'He does now. Or he rented one.'

That would probably be it.

What was so urgent that Lucien had to leave his best friend's wedding?

Chapter Sixteen

The communal door was wide open when I made it to Clapham. I took the lift as I had done six months ago, where I came to this apartment uninvited, where Lucien had guests over. Jan wasn't there, and I wondered if Lucien had told him about the whole thing. Jan didn't give me the address, which gave me the impression he knew I had been there.

I puffed my cheeks before knocking on the door and checking my watch. It was precisely seven p.m.

A whoosh of chill-out music with an Arabic melody greeted me, and his strong cologne was like a slap on the face. He wore a plain black long-sleeve shirt with a chunky Indian-inspired necklace on his chest. His hair fell lusciously on his shoulder, exposing the shaved side.

'Hello, Emily,' he purred, opening the door wider.

His apartment had some of the most stunning furnishings I had ever seen. I imagined he spent a fortune decorating. It was like I had stepped into another exotic world. It had a Middle Eastern influence, and the smell of incense whiffed into my nostrils. The last time I had been there, there was a portrait of himself above the fireplace.

Now it was gone, and in its place was an empty space. Maybe he thought it was vain.

'Anything to drink?' he asked.

'Water,' I said.

He glanced back at me, frowning. 'Come on now, Emily.'

Without giving me a chance to reply, he swaggered to the next room, which I assumed was the kitchen. He returned moments later and handed me a goblet. It made me feel like a maiden in medieval times.

'Jan,' I said.

'Yes?'

'What is this about?' I asked.

'Your detective came back asking questions.'

My detective? It ticked me off, this comment. Jan knew I had a brief fling with Ben as I told him in the hospital so he would get the complete picture of what Travis had done. I knew what Jan was doing, but I wasn't going to give him the satisfaction.

'What did he want?'

Jan sat down on the sofa. 'He asked more questions about that night. Has he come to ask you questions?'

'Not yet, but I have a feeling he might.'

'You can have a seat, you know,' he said.

'Oh yes,' I said and sat on the armchair away from him.

A line had been crossed that shouldn't have, and I was trying to keep this as grown up as possible. It only takes one sip of that glass filled with promise, and it would lead you to do something you didn't usually do, and it would be too late to undo it.

'And did you…?' I trailed off, sighed and tried again. 'Did you tell him about what you saw?'

He looked at me sharply. 'What I saw?'

'That morning before you came to the room.'

'No, I didn't.'

I furrowed my eyebrows. 'Why not?'

'Because,' he said. 'I'm not sure what I saw. There are cameras. I'm sure they will catch whoever did this in no time.'

Maybe it wouldn't be that simple.

'Olivia requested an audience this afternoon,' I announced.

'Oh really? What did she want?'

'She's worried for Lucien. Have you heard from him?'

'No, his phone is off, and he disabled his accounts again.'

I looked at him, astonished. 'He has?'

'Yes.'

'Why?'

'He doesn't want to be found, I guess.'

But if he disabled the accounts, that meant he was all right, and he simply didn't wish to be tracked on any apps.

'But this is so unlike him, taking off without telling anyone.'

'It is,' Jan admitted. 'But people change.' His blue, jewel-like eyes flicked in my direction. 'And he has.'

It was like he was saying I was responsible for this introduction to the new Lucien. Maybe I was. I let this hang in the air.

'A neighbour told me she saw Lucien the night of the wedding,' I said.

This made Jan perk up. 'Oh, she did?'

'Yes, she said she saw him standing in front of Olivia's house.'

He raised an eyebrow. 'He was?'

'That's what she said.'

'He was standing there?' Jan asked in disbelief.

'Yes.'

'Odd. And then what?' he asked.

'He drove off.'

His forehead creased. 'Drove off? But Lucien doesn't have a car.'

'Maybe he rented a car. Do you know anything about him renting a car?'

'What, on a Friday night in the middle of the night? I would like the name of this convenient company.'

'You don't know anything about him renting a car?'

'No, we went to the venue in the car Sasha provided for us.'

'But he left at midnight?' I asked.

'That's what the police said. I wouldn't know. I was with you.'

I gulped my goblet as silence fell in the room.

'We were in the hotel room at midnight?' I asked.

'No, at the party,' Jan replied.

How could he be so sure when we were both off our tits? Something didn't feel right, but I didn't want to have suspicions about Jan. A thought came to me then. When I woke up the morning after, Jan wasn't in the room, but he came in after I had woken up. Where was he then? He must have left at some point and left me in the room to sleep off my hangover.

'So, you haven't heard from him?' I asked.

He glanced into his glass. 'No.'

'What about Cassie?'

'Cassie?' he asked.

'Yes, the girlfriend or whatever she is.'

Jan ran a hand through his hair. 'She's the first person I contacted.'

'And?' I prompted.

He crossed and uncrossed his legs. 'She claimed Lucien left her at the hotel and stayed at the wedding.'

'So, she spent the night there?'

'I don't know. I didn't ask. I remember vaguely seeing her when we left the room, but I can't recall where.'

'Do you remember why we left the room?' I asked.

Jan claimed he could keep his drink, and I was sure guys like him partied hard but never got that drunk that he blacked out. Now, he suspected our drink or drinks had been spiked.

'Do you know where I can speak to her?' I asked.

'Who?' he asked.

'Cassie. I don't want to reach out to her on social media.'

'You want to ambush her?'

'If need be, yes.'

He smiled mischievously. 'Aren't you the amateur sleuth, little Emily?'

'Name of a place you know Cassie likes to go?' I asked, ignoring his comment.

'She likes to go for walks in the forest.'

I stared at him. 'Which forest?'

'Not sure.'

I crossed my hands under my chest. 'Well, that's not very good, is it?'

He leaned forward. 'Cassie is a nature girl. It inspires her and makes her, you know… horny.'

I rolled my eyes as that picture of her and Lucien in the woods came into my vision.

'There is a café she likes to go to. It's by the woods. I can't remember the name, though.'

I scoffed. 'Did Lucien find out about us?'

He broke eye contact. 'No.'

'Why would he leave? He might have been upset about something.'

'Or he just left,' Jan suggested.

I stood and paced around the room, feeling the heat of Jan's gaze on me. 'There were two girls at the wedding.'

Jan inspected his nails. 'There were a lot of girls at that wedding. You have to be more specific.'

'They were both very beautiful, young, in your age group, I gather. One had black hair, and the other had long golden blonde hair reaching her waist. One was wearing a black nightie-like dress. The other wore a red corset with a tutu-like skirt. Does this ring any bells?'

He reached for his phone on the coffee table, and that was when something caught my eye. A pair of woman's panties. They were black and stringy. Jan caught me staring at them and made no attempt to remove them from sight or look embarrassed. I took a gulp of wine, and Jan turned his phone in my direction, where a photo of the girls came into view. They were at a festival, and there were people around them. The blonde was dressed in a grey dress with moon designs, stockings and high-heeled rubber-soled boots, her blonde hair cascading off her shoulders. The dark one wore the same-looking boots, a black corset with lots of buckles, a long black skirt with a slit reaching her thighs, and a tiara on her head.

'Are these the girls you're referring to?' Jan asked.

I walked over and squinted at the screen. 'Yes, those are the ones.'

'They are influencers,' he explained. 'Big in the alternative community. You can find them on my Instagram. They are tagged over there.'

'Ta.'

My eyes couldn't help to go back to the panties. Jan was frowning, and something about them seemed to perturb him.

'Is everything all right?' I asked.

He glanced at me. 'Yeah… um… I found those in the mailbox. It might be a woman taking a mickey.'

I stared at him. 'What do you mean you found them in the mail?'

He looked assumed by this. 'What, you got a G-string too?'

'No, but I got a note.'

His eyes darted back at me. 'What kind of note?'

'Hope you enjoyed the wedding, and there was a condom.'

His eyes went wide. 'Say what now?'

'It was… chilling.'

Jan looked at the panties with a fresh eye now. Was it a woman taking a mickey? Or was it someone who knew something and was trying to send a message? And who could it be? It was clear that someone was out there who knew we had been together. Was Lucien playing some twisted game with us? No, he was somewhere, and the police were looking for him.

'When did you get them?' I asked.

'This morning, you?'

'Last night. Did you check the mail last night?'

'No.'

'So, it could have been there from last night?'

He rubbed his face with his hands. 'Could be. How is the lovely Anna?'

'She's fine.'

'Have you told her about us?'

'No, and I'm not going to.'

'Keeping it a secret?'

'Yes.'

It was happening again. Someone was playing tricks on me.

'Do you have any idea who might have done this?' I asked.

'From my end…? Well… it could be anyone.'

'Because of your social following,' I commented.

He nodded.

But who would do this to me? Suddenly, the walls felt like they were closing in on me and my heart crashed into my ribcage, and there was a stabbing pain in my chest.

I stood abruptly. 'I need to go.'

He nodded again, stood, and walked me to the door. 'Can you tell me if you get something like this… again?'

'Yes,' I replied.

I hurried out of there, and once out in the cool air, I leaned against the wall. I placed my hand on my chest, feeling my heart thumping. I wouldn't be in this position if I stayed away from these beautiful but messed up people.

Chapter Seventeen

Their names were Yovanna and Apolonia. Yovanna was from Serbia, and Apolonia was from Poland. Both models and social media influencers. They had their own side projects, Yovanna, a graphic designer and photographer and Apolonia, a seamstress and a photographer, both vegan. Yovanna also had an OnlyFans account. I scrolled to Yovanna's feed first; all she had were professionally taken photographs. I went to the tagged tab, and there were images of her at festivals with people I didn't know and a few with Lucien, Jan, and Sasha. I went to Apolonia's profile next, and it was the same. I had to find out where they'd be; the only person to help me with that was Jan.

I went to Cassie's Instagram, but she hadn't posted anything new. The circle on her profile was flashing pink. Jan told me in the text that he wanted to find out what happened that night as much as I did and who sent him those panties, but I needed to do this alone. He could hinder his own investigation if he liked. I was trying to remove myself from models, stalkers, and troublemakers.

I resumed work, and at 3 p.m. I stopped to make myself a cup of coffee when the buzzer went off. Before I could see who it was, I saw the communal door open and close. I waited, my heart jogging against my chest. The knock came a few moments later. Reluctantly, I opened the door, and Sasha walked past me without saying a word.

She stood in my living room, taking it all in. The basic white sofa, the coffee table, and my desk, organised and professional with my notebook and notes. She wore a long black t-shirt and black and grey striped leggings. Her purple hair was up in a messy bun, and her face was free from make-up. I had never seen Sasha without make-up, and she wore lots of it. She had no eyebrows, making her look like a different person. There were dark circles under her eyes that looked like bruises, and the whites were red. She threw herself at me, wrapping her arms around my waist, and I could only stare at my curtains in confusion. What was she doing here?

The way to approach this was with comfort, but I didn't want to say everything would be all right when things clearly weren't. The man she thought she would spend the rest of her life with was dead. She was questioned by the police and was possibly a suspect. No, things weren't all right.

'Cup of tea?' I asked.

She sniffed and nodded.

I made her sit on the sofa while making a cup of tea for her and a coffee for myself. I handed her the mug of tea, and she cupped her hands around it. Her nails were like claws and painted with purple nail polish. She had delicate hands, I noted, pale and soft. A hand of an artist that wasn't accustomed to hard work.

'I'm very sorry for your loss,' I whispered.

Tears slid down her pretty face. I went to the bathroom to get her a roll of toilet paper. I handed it to her, and she tore handfuls of loo paper with her tiny hands and buried her face in them.

'I don't know why I'm here, to be honest, but it is the only place I could think of. Sorry for barging in like this. You must be busy,' she said.

'No, it's okay.'

I was busy, but I wasn't going to kick her out, and I needed all the information I could get from her about what might have happened.

'Where is Lucien?' she asked.

'I don't know,' I said gently.

She looked at me with scepticism. 'He didn't tell you where he went?'

'Why would he?' I asked.

'Because you're… oh, never mind. He probably fucked off to some festival.'

'Festival? After what you've been going through? That is a bit...' I paused, looking for the right word. 'Cold.'

If he went to a festival, they could track him, though.

'He became a different person after being released from the hospital. I know that what happened to him had fucked him up, but I am his friend,' Sasha reasoned.

'Have you spoken to Cassie?' I asked.

She nodded. 'She doesn't know where he went either.'

'Sasha, can you tell me what happened?'

'I don't know. I wasn't in the room when it happened.'

'Where were you?'

'I...' She hiccupped and started to snob again.

I stared into space, thinking of what Jan had said; he thought he had seen someone go in the room but wasn't sure who but could swear it wasn't Sasha because of her bright hair. Whoever came to their suite must have been watching it and knew Sasha wasn't in the room.

'Does anyone know you're here?' I asked her after she calmed down a little.

She shook her head and sipped her tea.

'Where are your parents? They must be worried.'

'I'm so fed up with them fussing around me and asking me the same questions over and over. They and the police all looked at me as if I had done something. I would never hurt him. I wasn't even in the room.'

'Okay, calm down,' I told her. 'You're under a lot of stress. Have you eaten?'

'Not much. Here and there. I haven't had much of an appetite lately,' she replied.

'Understandable,' I said.

'Would you mind if I lie down for a bit?'

She looked at me with big, pleading brown eyes, and I found it hard to say no to her.

'Sure, go ahead. We will talk later.'

She yawned and laid her head on the sofa, making herself comfortable, and I didn't mind. She needed a place where she felt safe, although I didn't know why she came here of all the places she might have gone to. Couldn't she have gone to her parents? Jan's? Olivia's?

I stood and let her rest while I took my laptop to the kitchen and worked there so I wouldn't disturb her. I could see her from where I sat, lying on the sofa, her head on the cushion, and her eyes closed. I made out the rise and fall of her chest, looking peaceful even though she clearly wasn't.

Chapter Eighteen

I made Bolognese sauce and let it simmer for at least three hours. Sasha had woken up and told me the smell of food woke her. I toasted the bread to make bruschetta to go with the pasta. Comfort food. It was what she needed, and I needed it as much as she did. She stood by the kitchen, asked if I needed any help, and I told her it was fine. She smiled, and she looked so young and innocent. She suggested we open a bottle of wine. I had a bottle of red wine sitting in the cupboard that Anna had bought with her when she came over, but we didn't open it. After what happened at the wedding, I was trying to avoid alcohol. It was ironic, given that I drowned my sorrows in the bottle a few months ago.

Sasha opened the red wine, sat at the kitchen table, and started eating. It was so strange to have her, of all people, sitting in my kitchen and having dinner. Had I ever done this with Lucien? I didn't think I had, but we didn't have that kind of relationship, although it would have been nice.

'How is Anna?' she asked.

'She's good. Trying to paddle on from… all of that.'

'I think of him, Travis. I think of him all the time. We welcomed him into our squad, and he did that to us and to me. Jan was so nice to him, sheltering him and Lucien without asking for rent. It was so classy of him. Never in a million years did I think he would do that to Anna. He was so soft and delicate.'

'You just don't know with people,' I told her.

'No, you don't,' she agreed. 'You seemed like you had a wonderful time at the wedding.'

'It was a beautiful wedding.'

'It was… I saw you briefly at the party dancing with Jan.'

I tried to be as casual as possible about this.

She placed her fork down and smiled. 'You know Jan fancies the pants out of you, right?'

'No, he doesn't,' I said.

'Oh yes, he does. He finds you lovely. That's how he describes you.'

I struggled to imagine I was being discussed, and there was I, thinking he was lovely.

'Hence why,' she said, 'he never slept with Anna. He is picky about the people he sleeps with.'

Was he? I wanted to laugh. He had slept with Sasha when she was in a relationship with Lloyd. That didn't seem like someone who was picky to me. He fancied me, and I made it so easy for him. I took a gulp of wine, saying nothing about this as I wondered what she was eluding to.

'I didn't know that.'

'Oh, come on,' she said. 'He teased Lucien, telling him he should have seen you first.'

'What did Lucien say?' I asked.

'To fuck off.' She twirled the spaghetti with a fork. 'What do you think of him?'

'Who?'

'Jan, of course.'

Why was she asking me this? What did he tell her? What did she know?

'I think he's the most stunning person I have ever encountered,' I admitted.

'More than Lucien?' she asked.

I looked down at my food. 'They are both stunning in their own way.'

'Yes,' she agreed. 'They are. Bastards.'

I smiled and let the quiet fall between us.

'They thought I pushed him, but I wasn't even in the room,' Sasha said.

I glanced at her. 'Where were you?'

'We stayed for the party for about an hour, then we went to our room, and you know... we consummated the marriage, then we left again and partied some more. We went back to our room and got at it again. Neither of us felt sleepy, so I suggested we dip in the indoor pool. He told me he would join me, so I left and went for a swim. The camera proved that, but it took a while for the police to get hold of it.'

'Don't they have the footage of who might have gone into the room?'

'Nope, only the one in the indoor pool,' she said.

'What do you mean?'

'Apparently the camera on our floor wasn't working that night.'

'How convenient,' I said.

'Yes, very,' she said.

That meant whoever went into the room after Sasha knew the camera wasn't working, or it could have been a stroke of luck. I stood, cleared the plates away and put the kettle on. I leaned against the counter where Sasha was scrolling through her Instagram.

'Can I ask you something?' I asked.

Sasha placed the phone down on the table. 'Of course.'

I sat back down on the chair. 'That night of the wedding, did you see me outside the hotel?'

'Um… I can't say I did.'

'You never saw me?'

'No.'

'What about Lucien?'

'He just left. I don't know why. Did you say something to upset him?'

'No,' I said.

She narrowed her eyes at me. 'Or maybe he saw something?'

'What could he have seen that would upset him at a wedding?' I asked.

'You tell me.'

'Sasha, do you know something I don't?'

'Look, I saw you dancing with Jan, laughing and having a good time. You looked happy, and I'm glad that you were. You've been through a lot, like all of us have. What you did afterwards with Jan is none of my business, and I assure you, Lucien, of all people, wasn't going to leave my wedding and leave the country because you were getting lovey-dovey with Jan.'

How many people had seen me? There were people there who knew me, but I didn't know them, and with mobile phones these days, anyone could have snapped a picture and sent it to him. But Jan and Sasha said Lucien wouldn't be upset about it. When I was having my fling with Ben, Lucien wasn't all that pleased about it. He had made a few remarks and even admitted he was jealous. I had to find out what happened that night, and then I'd worry about Lucien's feelings later. I stood and made the coffee.

'What about Cassie?' I asked, changing the subject.

Sasha cupped her hands around the mug. 'Cassie is one of my best friends. She's part of our squad.'

I sat across from her. 'So… Lucien knew her for a long time?'

'Yes. They hooked up here and there. It's very casual. He has been living with her until he figures out what to do next.'

'Is there a way I can speak to her?'

'I'm sure it wouldn't be a problem.'

I had to ensure it would be somewhere public, not in a forest.

'Why do you want to speak to her, if you don't mind me asking?' Sasha asked suspiciously.

'Lucien.'

'Oh, of course. I'll fix you up.'

'How?'

'Oh, leave it to me,' she said.

I stared as she typed on her phone. She could have been sending her a text right that instant.

'Sasha, put the phone down,' I told her.

She looked up and placed the phone down face up this time, and I saw the chat was open and she was going to send a text to Cassie.

'You know that Lloyd's death was no accident, right?'

'Yes, I'm aware of that. I would like to find out what happened. Who would do this to me, to him, to us? And why?'

'I can help you.'

She looked at me suspiciously. 'Why?'

'We had our difficulties in the past, but I think you're an extraordinary young woman, and something happened to me that night too.'

'What happened?'

'I blacked out, and so did Jan, and he thinks our drinks might have been spiked.'

She threw her hands to her mouth. 'Oh my God. Why?'

'I have no idea. Didn't he tell you?'

'No, I didn't have the time to speak to him properly. That is terrible. Who would do that?'

'I have no idea, but someone who was at the wedding.'

'There were ninety people at the wedding.'

'Now, if Jan is correct, if someone did, in fact, spike our drinks, it could be the same person who pushed Lloyd. Had you blacked out?' I asked.

'No,' said Sasha, 'I had a lot to drink, but not to the extent that I blacked out. Is that why you want to speak to Cassie?'

'I just want to know what she saw.'

'The police have already questioned her, and she wouldn't do something like this.'

'Well, nobody thought that Travis would do the things he did, and here we are.'

'But she's different,' she argued. 'She's my friend. She wouldn't do that. I know her.'

'I'm not saying she did it. Also, there were two girls at your wedding.'

I thought about how to go around this without letting Sasha know I had been at Jan's place and that he had already told me who the girls were and that I had looked them up. I played the dumb card and explained to her their dresses, and just like Jan, Sasha went to her Instagram and turned her phone, so I could see. This image was different from what Jan showed me. Sasha was with them where they were in a festival dressed in black and leather.

Sasha told me there an event coming up that weekend where Yovanna and Apolonia were going to be, and Sasha was going to take me.

Chapter Nineteen

I met my parents for dinner. Although I was cheery around them, I hadn't been myself since I moved to the house in Greenwich. My life had been flipped upside down, and now I was trying to find a balance, but each time I tried to do that, I turned around, and something had to happen, a mishap or a mistake. I thought of Lucien and where he could be, thinking of what he'd told me in the past that might lead to a clue. He sold all the properties, moved out and lived with Cassie. Did she know where he was? I think the police had questioned all the guests, all ninety of them. Why did Lucien flee? Had he seen something and got scared? Did something happen? He checked out at midnight. Where was he? I couldn't help but worry.

'Are you all right?' Mum asked, snapping me out of my thoughts.

'Just tired,' I lied.

I was tired of the mess that came with that group of beautiful people who brought nothing but despair. I felt like I was looking at myself outside the restaurant window, not completely in the moment.

'Why don't you come over for lunch this Sunday?' Dad asked.

Sasha was still at my apartment, and I asked myself what she was doing in there alone. Was she looking at my things, opening cupboards and drawers, learning new things about me? Would she go on my laptop? Look at my search history? My laptop was password protected, but that didn't make me feel secure.

'I'll see what I can do,' I said.

'You work too hard,' Mum said. 'You deserve a break.'

#

In the morning, I woke up to find Sasha was already awake making coffee. She was still dressed in the same outfit, and I couldn't help to notice how weak and frail she looked. I asked her if she had found anything yet, but she said she hadn't.

'Sasha,' I told her. 'You have been staying here for days. Do you have a change of clothes?'

'I don't want to go back to the apartment. It's filled with memories of him.'

'But aren't your parents there?' I asked.

'No, they left for Dorset. The police don't want me to leave London for now,' she explained. 'You know, in case they need me.'

I wondered if she had spoken to Jan and if he had told her everything, most notably what he had seen on his way to the room. I was dying to ask, but if he hadn't mentioned anything to her, it would open a can of worms. If there was someone who should tell her about what he saw, it was him.

'I'll come with you. Would that help?' I offered.

She nodded.

We drank our coffee in silence, me on my feet gazing out the window, where I watched a mother prepare her children for school. *Will I ever be like her?* I thought. *Will I ever have children?* It wasn't too late. I still had time. Rain drizzled outside as I watched the mother escort her children to the car before driving them to school.

'Emily!'

I turned. 'Yes?'

Sasha was still sitting around the kitchen table.

'I noticed you don't have a single photo in this apartment. Shouldn't you have a few with your parents or Lucien? Anna even?' she asked.

This question took me back to Lucien's old apartment, where he had pictures displayed. Did he still keep pictures now? After all that he went through? Did he have photos with his parents after what they did to him? Of Sylvain?

'Um… Lucien and I were never a couple,' I said.

114

There wasn't an occasion that he or I took a picture together to collect as a memento. Why should we take pictures as if we were a loving couple? I thought of when I used to take many pictures with Ed, but that was the old Emily. A woman who I did not recognise.

Sasha opened her mouth to say something, but I didn't want to hear it.

'The weather is terrible,' I said. 'We should go to your place before it gets worse.'

She blinked at me, then nodded.

#

Sasha shared a loft with Lloyd in Camden; everything was thrown in one space. A kitchen with an L-shape counter, a living room with large windows overlooking the canal, and a bedroom. There was a lot of artwork on the wall. Sasha moved around the bedroom, picking random outfits as I moved around the living room. On the cabinet were photographs in frames; one of them was of Sasha in a big black Victorian-inspired dress. There were a few with Lloyd and with what she liked to call "the squad." The photo must have been taken with a selfie stick. There was Jan, Lucien, Lloyd, a blonde girl I did not know, and a dark-haired one. I moved to the next one, and someone had taken this photo. They were the same bunch with more dark-haired girls, but one stood out, Cassie. Everyone was looking at the camera except Cassie, who was glancing at someone in the front, and it seemed like she was looking at Sasha. I glanced towards the bedroom; Sasha wasn't there. She must have gone to the bathroom to collect more items from there. I quickly took out my phone and took a picture.

Sasha came out of the bathroom holding a blue duffle bag.

'All done,' she announced.

'You seem like the type of people who have lots of fun together,' I said, pointing at all the pictures.

Sasha glanced at them. 'Oh yes, we do. Gosh, I don't know how we made it from one party to another.'

'You party a lot?' I asked.

'Oh yes, too much. Shall we?' she asked.

'Of course.'

'Let's get lunch. It's on me,' she said and linked her elegant arms in mine. 'I insist.'

#

Lunch was at a sushi restaurant in the neighbourhood. Sasha confessed she loved sushi so much that she would have it every day if she could. I let her order for me, and she ordered many items, and what we didn't eat, we could always take it back with us, she said.

'How did you all meet?' I asked her after the sake was poured.

'School, festivals, and mutual friends. I've known Lucien since he moved from Exeter. I met Jan at a festival. He was there with his dad.'

'Jan was at a festival with his dad?'

'Yes, he has the coolest parents. I wish my parents had taken me to festivals. They live in a camper van and travel all around. We went with them once. It was brilliant,' she explained excitedly.

'We who?'

'Jan, Lucien, the other two girls from our group and me.'

'And you lived in a van, all of you?'

'It's equipped with a shower and everything. Can you imagine travelling for weeks without access to a shower and smelling each other? Gross.'

She wrinkled her nose at the thought.

I smiled. 'How did you meet Lloyd?'

She gazed sadly at the window.

'Sorry, I didn't mean to—'

'It's fine,' she said. 'At a festival, actually. He was drunk, and I bought him food. He said I saved his life.'

She smiled while she recounted this. 'We hooked up after that. Did you have lots of friends when you were at school?' she asked.

'Um… yes, but they all moved on. They got married, had kids, or moved to live elsewhere. Anna is the one who stayed.'

The waiters arrived with many plates, and Sasha clapped her hand excitedly. I thought she was like a child, and I wondered how long she would stay with me.

Chapter Twenty

After I stored the sushi in the fridge, Sasha announced she was going to meet a friend for drinks and asked if I would like to join. I told her I had to work, which wasn't a lie. I opened my laptop to show Sasha that I wanted to be alone and not be disturbed. This was understood as she went to the bathroom, had a quick shower and went to the bedroom, where she shut the door. I checked my emails, puffed on my cheeks and read through them. After ten minutes, I opened the tab and checked Lucien's social media accounts, but they were still disabled. If the police were looking for him, his socials were the first thing they would look at. Where was he? Was he all right? I tried calling him again, but his phone was off. What was going on with him?

I looked at the closed bedroom door and wondered what Sasha was doing in there. I stood and passed near the door and pressed my ear against it, but it was quiet. I opened the door without knocking. It was my apartment, and she was a guest.

Sasha was sitting on my dressing table, which I hardly used, holding an eyeliner wand. There was a make-up case that was open. She blinked at me as if to say, *paranoid much?*

'Don't close the door, please,' I told her.

'Okay.'

She was transforming into herself quickly, given it was days since Lloyd died. Was I going to judge a woman for wearing make-up and getting her hair done? People coped differently; this group wouldn't be caught dead without looking at least close to perfection. I made myself a cup of coffee and resumed work.

Sasha came out fifteen minutes later, beautifully dressed in a black Lolita-style dress, black tights, high-heeled boots, and a black bow sat prettily on her head.

'I won't be long. Just a quick drink, and I'll be back in a jiffy,' she said.

All of that trouble for just a drink? I thought.

'Have fun.' Then I cringed at my comment. It was wrong to say that to her, but Sasha didn't seem to mind as she smiled and left.

\#

There was a knock on the door, and I scoffed, assuming it was Sasha who had forgotten something, but Ben stood in front of me, and I froze. He looked handsome in an excellent navy-blue suit. A lump caught in my throat. Could I shut the door in a detective's face? Probably not. I had no choice but to let him in. I imagined this was the reason he was here. He was investigating this case, or he might have taken it from someone else, knowing who was involved. Alison wasn't with him, and I could picture him insisting he'd do this alone and seeing raised eyebrows from the perky blonde detective.

'I would like to ask you a few questions about the night Lloyd Lee died. Do you have a minute?' he said.

So formal, so grown up.

I stared at the floor as I opened the door wider for him and noticed a patch of fluff in the corner.

He looked around my homey small apartment sponsored by Ikea. I gestured for him to sit on the sofa, and the air was humid with tension. He had called and texted, and I never returned any of his calls, even after he figured out it was Travis who was sending Lucien and me the flowers, attacking Sasha and Anna and setting my house on fire. I didn't want to speak to him. I was angry and upset, and because he arrested Travis and helped Lucien, it didn't change the fact that he lied to me and made me look like a fool.

'Did you hear anything strange while you were in the room?' he asked.

'No,' I said.

'Okay, and what time did you and Jan get into the hotel room?'

God, he would ask these questions when I did not know. It was all murky, and it would look suspicious. I tried to dive into my brain, but all I got was Jan and me in the lift, kissing, and him nuzzling my neck before we made it to his room. Lifts had cameras, and the police must have checked them. Shame consumed my face. We even had it on camera going up in that room. I wanted to go to that hotel and burn that recording. I knew what Ben was doing. This was a trick to see if I would lie to him. Cameras would have the time and date on them.

'I'm not sure. I had lots to drink,' I said nervously.

He passed me a sardonic look. 'How much would you say you had to drink, Emily?'

Hadn't he asked this already?

'Quite a lot.'

He glanced at his phone to consult his notes. 'At the wedding,' he went on, 'did you notice anything out of the ordinary?'

'No, everyone seemed to be having a good time.'

'Did you see Sasha and Lloyd at all during the wedding?'

'Er… yes. I did.'

'When?'

'During the ceremony, of course, and at dinner.'

'How did they seem to you?'

'Jolly, happy.'

'What about the after-party? Did you see them?'

'I can't say I did.'

He typed something on his phone, looked up, and his eyes bore into mine. 'Emily, just tell me where he is.'

'Tell you where he is?' I asked, although I knew who he was referring to.

'Lucien Jones or Winter, whatever you prefer to call him. Where is he?'

'I have no idea.'

He raised an eyebrow. 'You don't?'

'No.'

'But you two are... close, are you not? You, of all people, should know.'

'Well, I don't.'

'Perhaps,' he said, not trying to hide the bitterness from his tone, 'I've been mistaken. You are not that close to Lucien since you spent the night with his best friend.'

It wasn't a question, but a statement. He would bring it up. Of course he would, but I didn't have to explain myself to Ben. I was a single woman, and I wasn't in a relationship with Lucien. I owed nothing to anybody. Having sex with Jan might have been immoral, dumb and foolish, and I wouldn't have acted on it if I had been sober. I opened my mouth to speak, but Ben spoke before me.

'You didn't deny it, Emily. I have it here in writing from both you and Jan.'

'What do you want from me?'

'The truth. Just tell me where Lucien is. I'm not going to arrest him. I just need to speak to him.'

'I told you. I don't know where he is!' I snapped and jumped up from the sofa.

I headed to the front door and opened it for him, indicating he should leave. He stood, pocketing his phone and buttoned his jacket. I crossed my hands under my chest as anger rose like acid.

'You know what?' I said.

Ben turned to me and waited.

'How dare you come to my home and do this to me?'

'I'm only doing my job, Emily. You know this.'

'You are married, Ben, and you didn't tell me!' I shouted. 'You're a copper. I expected better from you.'

He gave me a sad look and said, 'Being a copper doesn't mean I'm good, or that I'm not allowed to make mistakes. There are a lot of bad cops out there.'

'Yes, apparently so,' I reasoned.

'I called you and sent you texts, and you shut me out, and you didn't give me a chance to explain.'

'What's there to explain? You are married, and you didn't tell me. That's why we are where we are.'

'It's more complicated than that,' he said.

I pointed my finger, meaning he should leave.

He stepped out and turned. 'What are you doing, Emily? Mixing yourself with these bad influences and sleeping with them? I thought you were better than that.'

He was one to talk. Without saying a word, I shut the door in his face.

Chapter Twenty-One

The event was going to take place in an abandoned warehouse in Camden. Neon lights flashed outside, and there was a black carpet. As we went inside, we were swallowed into the cold air. Rock music was bumping on the speakers, and the room was crowded with people dressed in black. Sasha kept her head low as she walked to the bar. Her hands were clutched into fists, and she seemed nervous, as if she didn't want to be seen or recognised by anyone. She handed me a purple drink which was too sweet. I turned, facing the room, and made out Yovanna and Apolonia sitting behind a long table signing merchandise.

'I didn't know they're… so well known,' I said to Sasha.

'They are. Come, let me introduce you,' Sasha said.

I followed her to the table; they looked so beautiful it made everyone around them irrelevant. Lucien surrounded himself with these stunning women and men and wanted to be with me. Where was the logic in that? Did I want to be with him after the chaos he had brought into my life? Maybe I should move out of London and start over in a country somewhere far away where I can find balance.

When Sasha approached, they all at once stood as if the queen had walked to their table. They rushed over and enveloped her with hugs. They expressed how sorry they were and how devastating this must have been for her. After five minutes of me standing there awkwardly, Sasha extended her hand to me, and the girls looked at me. If they recognised me, they didn't show it.

'This is my friend, Emily. Emily, meet Yovanna and Apolonia,' Sasha said.

'Hello, Emily,' Apolonia said, giving me a friendly wave.

Yovanna simply watched me. 'So, you're Lucien's muse?'

I didn't know what to say.

Apolonia's eyes went wide with recognition. 'Oh, now I remember you. You're the foxy lady from the picture.'

Lucien had taken photographs of me and described me as a foxy lady. It seemed like a lifetime ago when he'd shared that photo of me on Facebook.

Sasha laughed. 'In the flesh.'

'And you were at the wedding?' Yovanna said in her heavily accented voice, almost accusingly, as if I had no business being there.

'Yes, I was,' I said. 'Is there somewhere we can talk privately?'

Yovanna and Apolonia glanced at Sasha as if they had been ambushed. Sasha gave them a pleading look.

'Not now, though,' Yovanna said impatiently. 'We are in the middle of work.'

In my line of vision, I made out someone who didn't quite fit in there as much as I did. Dressed in a grey suit and blonde hair. It was Alison. What was she doing here? Did she follow us? Were the police keeping tabs on Sasha, and if she was staying with me, would that make me involved somehow?

I pressed my hand against Sasha's arm. 'Alison is here?' I whispered.

Sasha looked almost afraid. 'What?'

'I just saw her walk past.'

Sasha looked around. 'What is she doing here?'

'Trying to solve who killed your husband.'

'I can't be seen here. It wouldn't look good. We have to go, now!' she hissed.

Yovanna and Apolonia were back at their tables, signing stuff. Sasha made me turn around and walk to the door. I glanced over my shoulder and saw Alison approach Yovanna and Apolonia's table, taking out something from the inner pocket of her jacket. They looked at each other and stood.

#

We came face to face with Jan as he was about to walk into the club. Sasha grabbed him by the arm and pulled him so fast and hard that he nearly tripped, which was hilarious. Once on the street, Sasha let him go, and he adjusted his jacket.

'What is going on?' he asked.

'We had to leave,' Sasha explained.

'Why?' he asked in disbelief.

'The detective. I don't want to be seen in there. It wouldn't look good,' Sasha said.

'And why were you there?' Jan asked.

'I wanted to speak to Yovanna and Apolonia,' she said.

Jan passed a glance at me, knowing this was my idea. He turned his attention back to Sasha.

'Emily put you up to this?' he said.

'She told me about you two blacking out, and I have to find out who killed Lloyd.'

'Let the police solve that,' Jan argued.

'Like hell I will, and where the fuck is Lucien? He better not come here, or I will kill him myself!' Sasha shouted.

'Keep your voice down,' said Jan. 'And there will be no killing of anyone. Nobody knows where he is. I even asked Olivia, and she has no clue.'

'Great. Just great,' she said and stomped off.

Jan glanced at me. 'I didn't know you and Emily had become friends.'

He intentionally emphasised the word *friends*.

'She's staying with me,' I said.

He gaped at me. 'Let me get this straight. Sasha is staying with you at your apartment?'

His tone was incredulous. A group of people dressed in black who were talking too loudly walked past us and entered the club's direction.

'Yes,' I replied once the group was out of earshot.

'Why would she do that?' he asked.

I pointed my finger in Sasha's direction, who was still walking. 'She's over there. Ask her.'

Frowning, he walked off, following his friend. They were chatting about Lucien, where he might be, and the murder.

Then Sasha turned to Jan. 'Why didn't you tell me you blacked out?'

He placed his hand on her arm. 'Let's go to the pub and talk.'

We looked way overdressed for the pub. They didn't seem to care as they crossed the street to the pub. Jan held the door for us, Sasha went in, and as I was about to go in, he leaned in and whispered.

'You look especially scrumptious tonight.'

'Behave,' I said.

He let out a throaty laugh as I felt holes burning in me. Sasha was by the bar buying drinks as I picked a table in the corner. Jan sat across from me and rested his arm on the chair.

'Can't you think of a place where Lucien might be?' I asked him.

'No,' he said.

'But you're his best friend,' I reasoned.

'Yeah, so? That doesn't mean he tells me everything.'

'I'm getting worried now. What if something happened to him?'

Jan looked slightly amused. 'Like what?'

'Here we go,' Sasha said, placing a pint for Jan and two glasses of wine for us.

She took a seat next to me, and Jan observed us.

'Why Emily?' he asked.

Sasha and I glanced at each other.

'What do you mean?' Sasha asked.

Jan glanced around the bar. 'Why stay at her place?'

'Because I don't want to stay in the loft. It has too many memories,' she explained.

'You can stay with me,' Jan offered.

Sasha fingered the rim of the glass. 'I wanted to be around someone who knows what it is like, and you're not a woman.'

He wasn't pleased with this response. 'And you think I don't know what it is like?'

'No offence, Jan, but nothing happened to you,' Sasha said.

Jan's face darkened. 'Nothing happened to me? Are you serious?'

He was raising his voice, and a few heads were turning in our direction. We had to avoid any kind of conflict. A group of people arguing would leave an impression.

'Keep your voice down,' I hushed.

He glared at me, then averted his gaze back to Sasha. 'Don't tell me to keep my voice down. My friend was in a hospital bed after he got shot. Now, he's gone, and I have no idea where he is, and I blacked out at your wedding. At your *wedding,* at of all places. And you know me, Sasha, I never black out.'

'Okay,' she said. 'I'm sorry. Emily told me you suspect someone spiked your drinks?'

'Yes,' he replied.

'Can you walk me through what happened?' she asked.

I reached for my glass of wine and slurped it. Sasha cast me a sideways glance while Jan explained to her the same version of events leaving out the part of us going in a hotel room. Him finding the panties, and me finding the note. Nor about seeing someone walking into the suite.

'Where did you wake up?' she asked after he finished.

He adjusted his jacket. 'In the street. It was humiliating.'

'And what? Did you walk back to the hotel? That makes little sense, Jan,' Sasha remarked.

'I know it doesn't,' he said.

Sasha turned to me. 'And what about you? Where were you when you blacked out?'

My phone buzzed then, which saved me. It was Anna telling me she had come around, but no one was there.

'I remember being outside at some point,' Jan was saying. 'It was confusing, and I can't work it out. Do you remember anything else?'

This question was directed at me.

I glanced at him. 'No.'

Sasha was looking at me, then at him. 'Did something happen between you two?'

'No. Why do you ask?' Jan asked.

'I don't know… why would someone spike your drinks at my wedding? It seems like someone targeted you,' Sasha pointed out.

'Of course they targeted us, but why?' Jan asked.

'Maybe someone didn't want you to see something. Emily, where were you when you woke up?' she asked.

Panic surged through me, and sweat broke on my back. What was I going to tell her? Did she know I spent the night at the hotel? If I told her I woke up in a room, she would find it suspicious because she did not book a room for me. The hotel must have been booked solid that night.

Another text came through, and I reached for my phone.

'There are a lot of missing pieces in both of your stories,' Sasha was saying.

It was Olivia.

Lucien has been found.

Chapter Twenty-Two

'Lucien has been tracked down,' I announced.

Jan and Sasha gaped at me.

'Where?' they said at once.

'I don't know,' I said and showed them the text from my phone.

Jan's phone beeped, and he took it at once and showed us his text from Olivia saying the same thing.

'The police tracked him down?' Sasha asked.

Without saying a word, Jan stood with the phone pressed to his ear as he strolled out of the pub. Sasha and I waited, taking sips from our drinks.

'I hope he's all right,' Sasha said.

'Me too,' I said.

Jan walked in, sat across from us, and ran his hand through his hair. 'Apparently he took a flight to Berlin.'

'Berlin?' I asked.

What was in Berlin? This was news to me. He mentioned nothing of importance unless there was a festival, but would he still go to a festival when his best friend's husband had just died?

'What's in Berlin?' I asked.

'I don't know,' Sasha said.

'He didn't tell you he was flying to Berlin?' I asked.

This question was for both of them.

Sasha looked at me. 'I was hoping he would have told you.'

Why did everyone think Lucien would come running telling me things when we weren't even a couple?

'No, he didn't,' I said. 'Why does everyone seem to think he would tell me?'

'Because you are his muse,' Sasha declared.

'Nonsense,' I said. 'Is there a festival?'

'No, not yet,' Jan said. 'The next festival is in summer.'

'I feel like I'll be asked to go to the police station soon,' Sasha said.

'Why?' I asked her.

'Answer more questions, of course,' she replied.

'You can always get a solicitor,' Jan pointed out.

'If I get a solicitor, that would mean I have something to hide, Jan,' she said.

'No, it means you are protecting your arse. Everything you say can be held as evidence. Hiring a solicitor is the smart thing to do,' Jan advised.

'I don't have the money for a solicitor,' she cried.

'Then I'll loan you the money,' he said.

'Don't be ridiculous. You've done enough already,' she said.

I stood. 'I should go.'

Jan and Sasha looked up at me.

'Where?' Jan asked.

'Home,' I replied and looked down at Sasha. 'Are you coming?'

She reached for her bag. 'Yes, I'll come with you.'

Jan fingered the rim of his pint. 'Look at you, acting like roommates.'

'Jealous?' Sasha teased.

'Oh, very,' he purred.

We left Jan there as he met with a few people he knew. As we walked the route to the tube, I got the distinct feeling that Jan wasn't thrilled with Sasha staying with me, and I wondered why.

#

I stood outside the hotel where the wedding occurred as people strolled past me while I stared at the building. I thought this was an excellent place to start since this was where it all began. I was reluctant, however, to go in. I couldn't see the rooms since I hadn't booked one, but maybe I could ask the staff if they knew or had something, although they had likely already been questioned by police.

I puffed on my cheeks, walked in, ignored the front desk, and knew where I was going. I located the bar and sat down on the stool. There didn't seem to be a barman, and then a woman appeared from under the bar.

'Oh, hello,' I said.

'Hi, sorry about that. How are you today?' she asked.

'I'm… good, thank you.'

She seemed attentive and friendly. Maybe she was on shift that night. The name tag on her chest read Becky.

'What can I get you?' she asked.

'Um… gin and tonic. Thank you.'

'Any gin?'

'Yes, any will do.'

She smiled and busied herself making my drink. Two men in suits walked in and sat at the table.

'Here you go,' she said, presenting me with the drink.

'Um… may I ask, were you on shift on Friday the twelfth of May? There was a wedding here…' I trailed off.

'When the groom fell off the balcony?' she asked.

'Yes.'

'You were here when that happened?'

'Yes, not in the room, but I was a guest.'

'I was here on duty. I was working at the other bar for the wedding, but then my colleague got sick, so I was swapped to this bar. I was here on the late shift around closing,' she explained, then paused, frowning slightly. 'Now that I recall, I remember you.'

'You do?' I asked.

'Yes, you were with a guy... well, I remember him more because he looked very distinct and gorgeous.'

Of course she would remember Jan.

'I came here to this bar with my friend?' I asked.

She raised an eyebrow, most probably wondering, shouldn't I remember all of this? I felt I needed to explain myself.

'Yes, you ordered drinks,' she said.

'So, we were alone the entire time?' I asked.

'Um... I'm not sure. I got busy then, so I couldn't keep track.'

'I had a bit too much to drink. You know how it is. It was a wedding, after all,' I said nervously.

She nodded, thinking I was another one who couldn't handle her drink. I took my purse and handed her a tenner. She thanked me and moved to the new customer that had just walked in.

I took a sip of gin and pondered what she had told me. Jan and I had left the party, that I remember. We went to his room and came down here to the bar. Why would we do that when there was room service? I assumed a hotel like this offered such a service. Were we planning to go somewhere? Back to the party, maybe? Did someone spike our drinks here in this bar? My memory was all confusing after I went to the room with Jan. Maybe it was the other way around. We left the party and got a drink here at the bar. Someone spiked our drinks, and we went to the room. I inspected the bar, and there were cameras, two of them. If someone drugged us here, it would be on camera, and the police might have seen it, but the police were investigating a murder, not a drugging.

I left the hotel and strolled in the neighbourhood, hoping something would come to me. The streets were quiet here, and I couldn't imagine a racket being caused without anyone calling the police. The street was filled with townhouses, rows upon rows of them. A man rode past me with a bike which startled me, and I gasped.

My head hurt as a memory jogged out of me. I saw myself in black and white faltering down the street in the dark, looking lost and somewhat bewildered, and someone was shouting something. What was that? A name. Someone was calling out a name, but it wasn't clear. Was it Lucien? But that couldn't be right. Lucien might have left by this point, but had he?

Someone walked past me, pushed me, and I fell flat on my face.

I looked ahead on the street. Had someone pushed me? Who?

'Emily, what are you doing here?'

Chapter Twenty-Three

I turned, and Ben stood a few inches away from me. He was alone, dressed in a light grey suit and a purple tie. Was he following me? But the hotel wasn't that far.

'What are you doing here?' I asked.

He frowned and walked closer. 'I'm sure you've been informed that Lucien has been found.'

'Yes,' I said.

'And you had no idea he was in Berlin all this time?'

'Look, I'm getting fed up with everyone thinking I know where he is. He is not my boyfriend. I am not his girlfriend,' I retorted.

He glared at me. 'Just someone you fool around with from time to time?'

'That is—'

'None of my business?' he interrupted me, taking a step closer. 'It is my business when the police are involved, and you can't stay out of trouble, can you?'

'It seems trouble is looking for me,' I replied.

'No, Emily, you are getting yourself in trouble because of the people you're mixing yourself with.'

'I'm not mixing myself with anyone. I was invited to a wedding and attended to be polite.'

He placed his hands on his hips, sighing, and looked at the pavement and then in the direction of the hotel.

'I think it's time you and I had a chat, don't you think?' he suggested.

'Unless it has to do with the case, we have nothing else to talk about,' I pointed out.

'We do, Emily. I have to explain myself. Let me buy you a cup of coffee, please,' he said.

I sighed dramatically. 'Okay, fine.'

\#

We sat in a café in South Kensington. Ben ordered two coffees, and we sat at a table by the window, waiting for the waitress to serve us the order. His phone rang, and he stood to get it, then returned as the waitress bought us the coffee.

'I hate how things ended between us,' he began. 'I like you; I really do.'

'But you're married?' I said.

'Separated.'

'What?'

'I'm separated, have been for a few years. Sue, my ex-wife, and I were trying to work out what to do. The issue was work, that I'm not home a lot.'

He was separated and kept a photo of his wife in his wallet.

'Is this supposed to make me feel better?' I asked.

'No, of course not. I just… couldn't help it.'

That was the same excuse I had come up with when I started my fling with Lucien. Oh, I couldn't help myself. Lots of strange things were happening, and he was beautiful and attentive.

'We don't live in the same houses anymore,' Ben said. 'When Travis sent Sue those photos, it struck a chord. Things would not get any better between us, so we divorced.'

'Any children?' I asked.

'No.'

'So, your wife filed for divorce because of me?'

'It was a long time coming, Emily. It has nothing to do with you. I should have told you. You had every right to know. It was a dick move on my part.'

I glanced at the window, feeling like shit. 'You should have. I didn't need that after what I was going through.'

'I know, and I'm so sorry.'

I wanted to leave, get out of there, go home and be alone. But Sasha was there, and I had no privacy. Maybe it was time for her to go back to her place, or to her parents, or with Jan. I needed my space to breathe.

'Is there something else you want from me?' I asked.

'Yes, I did a conference call with Lucien in Berlin.'

'Oh, so he's staying there?'

'According to his flight, he should land here in three days.'

Three more days, I thought.

'What did he say?' I asked.

'I can't disclose that with you, but is there something else you heard or saw that night?'

I fingered my cup. *Better to tell him. It might help with his investigation.* 'Jan and I woke up disorientated and suffering from memory loss from that night, and we think we had been drugged.'

Ben stared at me. 'And you're telling me this now?'

'I didn't think it was relevant at the time, but now that I think about it, maybe it was the killer who spiked our drinks. I don't know. I went to the hotel just now. I thought it would trigger something, and the bartender told me Jan and I had a drink there. Did you check the cameras at the hotel?'

'Yes, apart from two that weren't working from that week.'

So two cameras weren't working at the hotel. I wondered where the other one was located. I couldn't ask Ben, as he likely wouldn't tell me.

'Can you tell me if we were on those cameras?' I asked.

Ben glared at me and took out his phone.

'You two came into the hotel at around twelve-fifteen am. Right after, Lucien left. You went to the lift and went to Jan's room.' He peered at me, then looked down at his phone. 'You came out at one-thirty am, went to the bar, and had a drink. Normally, the bar would be closed, but it remained open since there was a wedding, and Sasha's parents had it booked to remain open for another hour. You had a drink there, then you two left the hotel, and you came back alone at around two-forty-five a.m. and went back to the room.'

Where did Jan go?

'Jan didn't come back until the morning,' Ben went on. 'Does any of this ring a bell?'

'You have all of that on your phone?'

'I have everything of anyone who was a guest at the hotel logged on here.'

'I wasn't a guest at that hotel.'

'No, but Jan was, and you slept in his room.'

'I woke up with bruises, and someone pushed me.'

He sighed and finished his cup of coffee. 'I think you two bit off more than you could chew, and you got carried away. This is something you have to figure out on your own. Lloyd wasn't killed until eight a.m.'

Ben stood.

'But… can you check if someone was at the bar and poured something into our drinks? It is a crime, isn't it, to drug someone without their consent?'

'Yes, it is,' he said.

Ben was about to leave but changed his mind, placed his hands on the table and leaned closer. 'A word of advice, Emily. Just leave it all behind, and let them go, Lucien and his friends. They are troubled people, and you're not like them. They are out of your league. And Lucien, there is something not right about that bloke. I told you this before, but I guess you have to figure that out on your own. Maybe after the obsession will dissolve.'

'At least he doesn't lie to me,' I said. 'And I am not obsessed with him!'

He leered at me. 'Every day, I come across the worst scum you could possibly imagine. Thieves, rapists, wife beaters, abusers, killers, you name it. This is what I come face to face with every single day, and I see bad things happen to good people.'

'What are you getting at? What does this have to do with Lucien?'

'What I'm telling you is, I know when someone rubs me the wrong way, and I'm sorry, Emily, I know you care a lot about him, and he might have taken a bullet for you, but there is something off about him. I just can't put my finger on what it is.'

I stared down at my empty cup of coffee. *Ben is jealous,* I thought, *bitter because he fucked everything up.*

'Because he's different, it doesn't mean there is something wrong with him,' I said. 'He didn't have an easy childhood to begin with.'

Ben sighed as if I were a lost cause. 'Just go home and live your life and find some peace. Again, I'm sorry for what I did to you. I just wanted to explain, that was all. Now I have to go back to work. Take care of yourself and think about what I said.'

He placed a twenty-pound note on the table, put on his sunglasses, and walked out. I watched him cross the street, get into an unmarked car, and drive off. If I ever saw Ben again, it would be in a police station, if it came to that. It was sad how things ended between us. If only he had told me the truth from the start, things would have turned out differently. It was a shame. I really liked him, but any possible future between us was tarnished.

Chapter Twenty-Four

It was evening when I rang the flat's buzzer and the communal door opened with a click. The front door was ajar, and Jan stood by the window, a cigarette dangling between his fingers.

'Well, isn't this a pleasant surprise?' he purred.

'I need to ask you a question, and then I'll be on my way.'

'Oh,' he said, coming towards me. 'Not staying?'

'Don't be ridiculous. Of course I'm not staying. What we did was the dumbest thing two people have ever done. What's wrong with us?'

'There is nothing wrong with us. We were just two people caught up in the moment.'

'We were off our tits.'

'Still with the guilt trip, I see? If this is about Lucien, I told you he won't care.'

'I feel like shit. I haven't slept in weeks. Maybe Lucien won't be arsed, but it was wrong on many levels.'

'I assure you he won't, and we're not married or anything. Stop stressing yourself out over nothing. Is this what you came to tell me?'

'No.'

'Would you like a drink then?'

'No, I don't want a bloody drink.'

He walked towards the drinks cabinet that had an assortment of alcohol. 'Oh, Emily, now you do like your booze.'

'Wazzack,' I said.

He laughed and poured himself a drink. 'You're hilarious.'

He made me sit on the sofa and sat beside me a little too close and placed his hand on my knee, and I jumped.

He smiled cheekily. 'What is this about?'

'I spoke to Ben,' I blurted.

Jan lit another cigarette. 'Oh, you're back with him?'

I gaped at him. 'How did you know about that?'

'I know a lot of things,' he said, holding my gaze.

'Lucien told you, didn't he? I'm going to kill him!'

Jan puffed on his cigarette. 'It seems everyone is out to kill Lucien these days. Come on, darling, what did he tell you?'

I gazed down at my hands, where my nails were bitten to the tip. 'We came to the hotel at twelve-fifteen am, right after Lucien had checked out. Then we went back down at around one-thirty am. We got a drink at the bar, and the bartender confirmed this and then we left. I came back alone at two-forty-five am. Where did you go?'

Jan mushed the cigarette on the ashtray. 'I don't know. You know I woke up on the pavement. Not my finest moment.'

'Anyway, I remembered something else. Someone pushed me when I was out in the street.'

'Where was I?' he asked.

'I don't know.'

'But why did we leave the hotel?'

'I don't know why we went to the bar to get a drink in the first place.'

'Did Ben tell you he encountered anyone while we were at the bar?'

I shook my head. 'He didn't say, and I didn't ask. Did you get any more parcels in your mailbox?'

He played with the lighter. 'No, nothing, you?'

'Nothing either. Oh, and Lucien will land in three days.'

'About time. Oh,' he said, placing his jewelled hand on my thigh. 'Cassie will be at a pub she likes to go to. Are you still interested in speaking to her?'

'Yes.'

He stood. 'I'll take you to her.'

'Now?'

'Yes, now. Unless you have other engagements?'

'No, I'm free.'

I thought of Sasha in my apartment as I followed Jan out and down the street. He drove a black Suzuki Swift, which was relatively modest for a model.

#

The pub was in Covent Garden. There were a lot of plants outside, with two pillars by the entrance. Inside it was wooden and dark, not very busy. I spotted her sitting alone at a table with a pint for company.

'Cassie, darling,' Jan said.

She looked up at him, and her eyes went wide with surprise.

'Jan, hey,' she said, standing, and they gave each other pecks on the cheeks. 'This is a wonderful surprise. You look stunning, as always.'

'You look lovely, too. Love your make-up.'

The whole Mac range was on her face, but she looked lovely. Her eyes flickered in my direction and she passed a glare at Jan, understanding what this was.

'What is she doing here?' Cassie asked him accusingly.

Jan laughed. 'Emily and I are good friends. Aren't we, Emily, love?'

'Oh yes,' I said, playing along. 'Since Lucien introduced us, we hit it off instantly.'

She raised an eyebrow. 'But you're Lucien's ex.'

Is that what he told her, that I was his ex?

'Oh, you know how we are,' Jan said.

'I'm going to get myself a pint. You want something, Emily?' Jan offered.

'I'll have a glass of white wine, and bring some peanuts, please,' I replied.

'Wine and peanuts and you, Cassie, a pint?' Jan asked Cassie.

She stared at her pint, clearly confused. 'Sure. I'll have a pint.'

I sat across from her, and she watched me placing my bag on the floor. She wore a black blouse with frills and had a gorgeous golden broach with a ruby pinned above her chest.

'You are really pretty,' she said.

'Oh,' I said, taken aback. 'Thanks. I love your broach.'

She fingered the broach self-consciously. 'Thank you.'

Unlike Sasha, who had long claw-like nails with nail polish, Cassie's fingernails were cut short, and she didn't wear any nail varnish.

'Lucien will be back soon, did you know?' I asked.

'Nope, I didn't. We haven't spoken since he fucked off,' she said scornfully.

'Oh, strange, given you are his girlfriend. That is how he introduced you, after all,' I pointed out.

She glared at me. 'What do you want, Emily?'

'Here we are,' announced Jan, placing our drinks and a packet of peanuts on the table and winking at me.

'So, where were we?" he asked.

'Jan, what is this? Why is she here?' Cassie asked him.

'Emily and I were in the area, and I know you like to come to this'—he gestured with his hands—'wonderful establishment for a drink, and we thought we'd drop by and say hello.'

She squinted at us and pointed her finger at him. 'Are you two sleeping together?'

What an odd thing to say.

Jan laughed. 'Where on earth did you get that idea from?'

'I saw you two getting hot and bothered at the after-party, and I saw you taking Emily to your room. I don't think you took her up there to show her your scarf collection, did you?'

What else did she see?

She took a long slurp of her pint, looking pleased with herself as if she had been waiting for this moment.

Jan's face darkened, and he placed the pint down on the table. 'Okay, Cassie, what else do you know? Emily and I were plastered.'

'Isn't that what you do best, Jan?'

She said this with a tone of resentment. Did something happen between her and Jan?

'No, I was legless, off my trolley, and I'm pretty sure someone spiked my drink. I suspect the drug was molly,' Jan said.

'Isn't E your favourite?' she asked

'I'm serious,' he snapped. 'I woke up on the pavement without any recollection of where I went or did.'

Cassie placed the glass down with a thud. 'Okay, this is what I know. Lucien was in a bad mood at the wedding.'

'He seemed fine to me,' Jan said.

'Oh, come on, Jan, he has been in a pissy mood since he was released from the hospital. I know what happened with Travis and with his parents was awful, but he became such a miserable sod. At the wedding, he looked like he'd rather been anywhere but there.'

'What happened?' I asked.

Cassie looked at me. 'We got into a fight.'

'About what?' Jan asked. 'He mentioned nothing about a fight.'

'You weren't there. You were at the bar or something. He was in one of his moods, so I thought I would stay out of his way. He didn't want to go to the party and was dead set on that. So, I told him I was staying. He told me to fuck off and left,' she explained.

'And then?' Jan asked.

'Then, he left the hotel, and I went to the party on my own like a loser hoping you'd be there, and when I got there, I saw you were with Emily by the bar, and you guys were drinking, I mean, looking like you were having one hell of a good time. I was jealous at some point,' she said.

Jan frowned, saying nothing.

'Why?' I asked.

'Oh, I thought Lucien would stay, not leave me there like a lemon,' she said. 'So, I left the party and went back to the hotel bar.'

'And you saw us go in the room?' Jan asked.

'Yes,' she replied.

'And how do you know I came back to my room?' Jan asked.

'Duh, you were causing quite a racket,' she pointed out.

'What sort of racket?' I asked, alarmed.

'Oh, nothing scandalous,' she purred. 'It's not like anyone had to call security or anything, but you were laughing hysterically, being tipsy. It was a wedding after all,' Cassie said, pointing her finger at Jan. 'You lifted Emily up and spun her around and went into the lift with her legs wrapped around you.'

I let him do that? Just how hammered was I? I felt my cheeks turning all shades of red. I was mortified. There was no use keeping this from Lucien. This might have reached him all the way to Berlin. All those people who saw us. How embarrassing.

'I did that? I don't remember that,' Jan said.

'Neither do I,' I said.

'I'm not surprised you don't. You guys were sloshed. It's like you were on one hell of a ride,' she said, taking a sip of beer.

'Did you tell Lucien any of this?' Jan asked.

'Tell Lucien, are you nuts?' she retorted. 'He didn't even bother to contact me. I'm pissed at him. What a donkey.'

I laughed. Having someone as regal as Lucien being called a donkey was hilarious. Cassie glared at me, not sharing my amusement. Lucien had pissed off everyone and had a lot of explaining to do.

'What about the police?' Jan asked.

'The police are more interested in who pushed Lloyd to his death than what you guys were doing. You were just two people behaving like twits. You didn't bother anyone and did nothing wrong. It's not like you are married or anything,' she said.

'What about afterwards?' I asked.

'Afterwards?' Cassie asked.

'We left the room at two-thirty am and went to the bar to get a drink,' I explained.

'Wow, after all that booze? You were on a roll,' Cassie commented. 'My evening wasn't as festive. Frankly, it sucked, so after you two went in the lift, I went to my room and slept. Are we done here?'

'Yes,' Jan said. 'We're done.'

'Good, because I have friends to meet, and I should be on my way,' Cassie said and stood, paid for her drink, and left.

Jan and I stared into space in silence. Someone laughed loudly, which made me jump, and the music came on.

'Jan.'

He rubbed his face with his hands. 'What?'

'How did Cassie know we went to your room?'

He leaned his back on the chair, gazing at the table. 'I think she put the two together.'

I looked at him. 'We made a spectacle of ourselves, that is true, but the bar is not even close to the lift. There was no way she saw all of that unless—'

'—Unless she spied on us,' Jan finished for me.

Jan and I looked at the pub door. She was very detailed about her story. It was like she was following our every move. This made my bones go cold. How much did she know and wasn't telling us? What else did she see?

Chapter Twenty-Five

I heard voices coming from my apartment when I approached the front door. Did Sasha invite people over without telling me? I put the key in the lock and opened the door.

'There she is!' Sasha announced happily.

Anna and Sasha were sitting on the sofa. On the coffee table was a bowl of popcorn and a bottle of wine that Anna must have bought along. I frowned as I surveyed the scene. Anna must have come over unannounced, and Sasha let her in. Sasha and Anna knew each other briefly, and since they had been attacked by the same man, they might have talked about their experience, but something about this bothered me. I didn't want Anna to know that Sasha was staying with me. I hoped Sasha had settled her affairs and was preparing to move back to her apartment. She had to go there at some point and couldn't avoid it forever.

'Where were you?' Anna asked.

'Had a meeting with a client,' I lied.

Now I was even lying to my friend.

'What brings you here?' I asked Anna.

'I hadn't heard from you, so I thought I'd come round to check up on you, and I found Sasha here,' Anna explained, giving me a what-the-fuck look.

Sasha checked her phone and stood. 'I'm going for a short walk. Is that okay?'

'You can do whatever you want, Sasha,' I said.

'I won't be long, thirty minutes tops,' she assured me.

'It's fine, Sasha.'

Sasha picked her coat from the hanger while Anna and I stared at each other as Sasha opened the door and left.

'What is going on with you? What is she doing staying at your place?' Anna asked.

'She had nowhere to go, so I'm letting her stay with me,' I said.

'She has plenty of places to go, Em. How about her own place? Her parents?'

'She showed up here out of the blue. What was I supposed to do? Tell her to leave after what she's been through? She just lost her husband.'

'Isn't she a suspect? How do you think that makes you look?'

'Like someone who is helping her.'

'Look, I understand you feel sorry for her, but those people are bad news. You shouldn't have gone to that wedding. I told you this.'

I walked to the kitchen and got myself a glass of wine. I returned to the living room, reached for the bottle of red and poured it into the glass.

'I don't need a lecture from you right now, and there is no point dwelling on what I should and shouldn't have done. It happened. There's no turning back.'

I flumped down on the sofa, exhausted.

Anna sat beside me. 'Each time these people come into your life, all hell breaks loose. You're better off.'

'You're the second person to tell me that.'

She stared at me, bemused. 'Who else told you that?'

I crossed my legs. 'Ben.'

Her eyes went wide. 'Oh.'

'What?' I asked.

'He's married!' she exclaimed.

'Separated now, getting divorced,' I corrected her.

She looked at me with scepticism. 'He told you that?'

'Yes.'

She took a sip of wine. 'Well, he should have known better. What a shit.'

I drained the glass of wine and poured another. 'I am the shit, Anna.'

She placed her hand on mine. 'No, don't say that. It's not your fault. You didn't know.'

'I slept with Jan!'

There was a stunted silence in the room as Anna processed this.

'Wait, you what?' she asked.

I stood. 'At the wedding, I was looking for you. I couldn't find you, and I went to the hotel bar, and he was there. You know what he's like, so I went to the stupid party with him. We had lots of drinks, and I... oh God.' I buried my face in my hands. 'I'm so, so stupid. I'm so sorry.'

She placed the glass down on the coffee table and stood, coming towards me. 'Hey, it's okay.'

'Aren't you mad?'

She pulled a face. 'Why would I be mad? Because I chatted with him on Facebook, went out with him for a drink once, then he disappeared from the face of the earth, and then we reconnected?'

I blinked at her. I thought she would get upset. She got mad when I tracked him down.

'Emily, after T…' She sighed and took a sip of wine. 'After Travis attacked me, it made me see things differently. You are a good friend, and I'm not about to fight over some gorgeous guy I didn't even kiss. God knows how often I get drunk and end up sleeping with guys. I'm mad because you didn't tell me the truth from the start. So you woke up in his room that night?'

I rubbed my forehead. 'Yes.'

'Have you remembered anything else?'

I filled her in about what I found out.

'So you think Cassie knows more?' Anna asked.

'I think so.'

She nodded.

'And Lucien?'

'The police tracked him in Berlin. He's coming back in a few days.'

'Does he know about you and Jan?'

'No, I don't think so.'

She nodded.

'Anna, did you see something while you were at the wedding that was strange to you?'

'No, nothing of the sort.'

She held her glass of wine, thinking of something.

'What?' I asked, alarmed.

She placed the glass down on the coffee table. 'Now that I think about it, there was something, but it could be nothing.'

I turned to her. 'What? What did you see?'

'Lloyd came over to the bar when I ran into my friend there, and I congratulated Lloyd. You know, the usual jazz. This girl walked up to him and asked me if she could steal him for a minute.'

'Was it Cassie? Did she have orange hair?' I asked.

'No, I'd never seen her before.'

'Do you remember what she looked like?'

Anna considered this. 'No, sorry, I have no idea who she was. He didn't even introduce me or anything. There were so many people at that wedding, and everyone wanted a piece of him. He excused himself, and they went to talk somewhere out of earshot, and they looked like they were arguing about something from their body language.'

'Can you at least tell me if she was blonde or a brunette?'

'No, she had black hair with a fringe. Tall and pretty.'

Who could it be? Anna tapped my knee. 'I have to go. Please don't wait too long to text me, okay?'

'I won't.'

She smiled and stood, and I did the same.

'And you're not mad with the Jan thing?' I asked.

'Nah, he's gorgeous and all, but not my type. I speak to him because he's cool. There is nothing there.'

I opened the door, and Sasha stood by the door, ready to knock. Without saying a word, Sasha walked past us. Anna and I exchanged glances as Anna blew me a kiss, and I shut the door, ready to have another sleepless night.

Chapter Twenty-Six

Olivia invited me over to her house for a chat. I had barely stepped foot in the neighbourhood when I saw Agnes Parker coming towards me, waving her hand. I wanted to groan, frustrated that she might have been by the window as usual and saw me. I thought maybe I could go into Olivia's house pretending I didn't see her, but that was too mean.

'It feels like ages since I've seen you,' she said.

'Yes, I have been busy so…'

'How are things? I never heard from that nice detective.'

I glanced at Olivia's house, and Agnes glanced over her shoulder to catch what I was looking at.

'I'm sure his business here is done,' I replied.

'But did you hear anything else?' she insisted.

'Um… no, not really,' I lied.

'What about Lucien?' she prompted.

'I haven't spoken to him.'

'But—'

The yellow door opened, and Olivia came out waving at me. Agnes glanced at her, then at me, aghast.

'Sorry,' I said apologetically. 'But I have to go.'

'I don't know why you bother with her,' Agnes whispered. 'She is so rude and uptight. Come over for tea when you have time, love.'

'Of course,' I said.

I waved goodbye at her and smiled as Olivia stood waiting.

'Old habits die hard,' she said as I approached her door.

In the hall were two large suitcases. Was she going somewhere? Olivia shut the door behind me, and I followed her to the kitchen.

'I'm sure Jan has filled you in on the latest developments,' she said, putting the kettle on.

I paused from taking off my scarf. 'Why would he?'

'He told me he would. You two became close after Lucien was shot.'

I pushed the chair and sat down. 'I wouldn't say close. Just friendly. It was a hard time.'

She opened the cupboard and paused, leaning over the counter. 'Yes, of course. Jan is just marvellous. I saw him grow up. Well, both of them and Sylvain. Still can't get over it. To be that young and have your life robbed from you.'

'Had you ever spoken to Amelia after what happened?' I asked.

She resumed taking out the cups. 'Never.'

'Henry?' I prompted.

'No, but he sent a few letters addressed to Lucien. I got another letter from him a few days ago, actually.'

Why would Henry write letters to Lucien when Lucien visited him in prison? But since he had been gone for weeks, maybe he got worried since I assumed Lucien didn't inform Henry about the trip. Henry wrote letters to see why he wasn't visiting and sent them to Olivia's address since it was his old house and Lucien didn't have a permanent address.

'Lucien told no one of this trip apparently,' Olivia went on.

'Why would Henry write letters if Lucien was visiting him in prison?' I asked.

Olivia held the teaspoon in mid-air, blinking at me. Judging from the reaction, this thought hadn't occurred to her. 'I don't know. Maybe he got worried. I haven't opened them. It's something that Lucien has to do. I'll keep them for him, and he will decide what to do with them.'

The kettle boiled, and she made the tea and placed a cup in front of me. 'I bought this delicious apple pie from the bakery down the road. I'm dying for a piece, you know, looking for an excuse. Care for a slice?'

My stomach grumbled at the mention of food. 'Sure.'

Olivia grinned, opened the fridge, took out the apple pie, and popped two pieces into the microwave.

'Ice cream or custard?' she asked.

'Just by itself, thank you,' I said.

Olivia served me the apple pie and placed hers with one scoop of ice cream and custard.

I thought of the luggage in the hall. 'Are you going on holiday?' I asked.

Olivia cut a big chunk of apple pie with her fork and popped it into her mouth. I took a sip of tea and waited as she chewed slowly.

'Yes, we are,' Olivia said, wiping her mouth with a paper napkin. 'We are going to California.'

'Wow, which part?'

'Los Angeles. My husband has a conference there, and he thought to make a holiday out of it.'

'Glamorous. How long are you staying?'

'Three weeks, it's long overdue. We haven't gone on holiday in years. What about you? Any plans to go on holiday?'

'No, nothing planned so far.'

'We'll be flying on Thursday.'

Two days after Lucien was due to come back.

'Hope you have a great time. Can I ask you something?'

'Sure, ask away.'

'What's in Berlin that Lucien felt he had to go there?'

'I don't know, Emily. He didn't tell me anything.'

'But does he have relatives there?'

'In Germany? No, not that I know of. Maybe he thought it was a good place to blow off steam.'

'So, he hasn't been in touch yet?'

'No, but I sent him an email that I would be away. Maybe he will drop by and visit. I really wish to see him before we go.'

She stood and cleared our empty plates. 'More tea?'

'No,' I said. 'I should be going.'

She checked her watch. 'Oh, I should go myself.' She placed the plates in the sink. 'You should come over sometime for Sunday lunch. It would be wonderful.'

'Sure,' I said. 'I would love to.'

As I left the house and looked at the empty space where my house used to be, I thought of the time when the phone rang in the early hours of the morning, of going there to find my house that I was already having a hard time selling, set on fire. Then Lucien got shot. It was the worst time of my life.

Now, I had been to a wedding with several hours of my life missing. I thought of what I had gathered so far, what Ben had told me, what Cassie had said, and I was sure she had followed us to the room. I thought of something else, the Post-it on the bin with hearts drawn on them. Did Jan draw them? He said he wasn't sure, but we were both drunk. If we hadn't done that, who did? Did someone come into our room? What about the note with the condom and Jan finding the underwear in his mailbox? Who sent those? What did it all mean?

Chapter Twenty-Seven

Sasha was sitting on the sofa when I walked into my apartment. There were fashion designs on the coffee table. I picked one up. It was a dress with a full skirt and bell sleeves.

'You like it?' she asked.

'Oh, these are wonderful,' I said as she shuffled through her designs. 'You are so talented.'

She smiled proudly. 'Thank you.'

I placed the design down. 'Sasha, there is something I have to—'

'I know,' she said, raising her hand. 'I overstayed my welcome, and I should let my butt out. I'm going back to the apartment. It's time.'

'That was not what I was going to tell you. Are you sure you're ready to go there by yourself?'

'I'm going to have a few friends over, and then my parents are coming to visit, and I made them promise not to drive me crazy.'

'That's because they love you.'

'I know. What did you want to tell me?' she asked.

I sat beside her, and she placed her notepad on the side.

'Anna told me during the wedding that Lloyd came up to her, and then a woman with black hair came up to him, and Anna said they looked like they were having some sort of argument.'

'Lloyd was arguing with a woman?' she asked.

'Yes, that's what she said. Does that ring any bells?'

Sasha thought for a moment. 'No, I was busy with the guests, the photographers and everything. Why would Lloyd argue with the woman at our wedding?'

'Was he in some sort of trouble?' I asked.

'Lloyd?' She scoffed. 'No. He would have told me if he was.'

Would he?

'Did Lucien take any pictures?' I asked.

'He did, yes, with his phone, I think. I'm not sure. You'll have to ask him.'

'Have you spoken to him?'

Sasha fingered her hair. 'Not yet, but I will.'

'I asked you this before, but are you sure you never left your room during the night?'

She shook her head. 'No, I didn't. It will come back to you.'

'What?' I asked.

'What you can't remember.'

I searched her face. 'Will it?'

'Maybe you should go and speak to someone.'

'A therapist, you mean?'

'Is it such a bad thing? I'm seeing a therapist to help me cope with everything. It helps. I can give you her number if you like. She's terrific. Maybe she can help you with the memories of that night, and you know, with everything else that happened.'

'I'm good, but thanks.'

She bit her bottom lip, looked at me as if she wanted to tell me something, and then stood. 'I'd better pack and get out of your way.'

'No, what were you going to tell me?'

She sat back down next to me. 'Maybe. Don't you think it's best not to remember? What if it's too awful?'

'I have to know, Sasha. I can't move on unless I do. Maybe I will get some sleep.'

She looked at me questioningly. 'I have pills for that.'

'I don't want drugs.'

'They're sleeping pills.' She smiled. 'My therapist prescribed them to me.'

'Not even legal drugs.'

'Did Jan do something to you?'

The question was so sudden it threw me. 'Jan?'

'Yeah, you were acting weird around him. Maybe it's a trigger or something.'

'I can't believe you would say that about your friend.'

She threw her eyes up. 'Emily, Travis was my friend, and look what he did to me. This experience made me quite distrustful of people. I'm sure you feel the same.'

'Yes, but…' I said. 'Jan is different.'

'Okay,' she said. 'But be careful.'

I booked her a taxi, although she told me I didn't have to as I had done more than enough. I insisted. Half an hour later, the taxi arrived, and I escorted her downstairs.

'You take care, okay?' she said.

'You too.'

'Call me if you need anything at all.'

She threw herself at me. 'He's very lucky to have you, and he's a loser if he doesn't see it.'

It's ironic how she called Lucien a loser when she called me the same thing when I ran to her at the tube and accidentally knocked my cup on her blouse.

She gave me a soft kiss on the lips, which took me by surprise. She backed away, smiled and got in the cab, where the driver was staring at us. I watched the taxi drive away until it disappeared around the corner. I stood there on the pavement for a minute or two, blinking rapidly before I turned to go back to a now empty flat. I opened my mail and frowned. Inside was a key.

Chapter Twenty-Eight

I sat down on the sofa, moving the key in my hand. It was just like any other key, nothing out of the ordinary, but who would leave me a key and why? Which door did it open? I logged into Facebook and searched for Lucien, but his account was still unavailable. Same with Instagram. I puffed my cheeks and considered my options. I checked Cassie's account. Her stories were mainly spooky images, and she posted a picture of a fruit basket. Her feed looked like autumn with a colour scheme of red, brown and orange. It was lovely, with pictures of a forest, her cats, and a picture of herself here and there. I left her feed, went to Jan's profile, scrolled into his tagged section, and looked for Yovanna and Apolonia's profiles. I went to Yovanna first. There was nothing apart from photoshoots.

I stood, went to the kitchen, and poured myself a glass of wine. I returned to the coffee table, and as I placed my glass down, I noticed a card. I picked it up. It was the name of the therapist and a contact number. Sasha might have left it there for me to use when needed. I thought about calling and asking if she could help me retrieve my memory of that night, but I had to answer many questions, and I was looking for a quick fix.

I placed the card down, took a large swig of wine, picked up my phone, and went to Apolonia's profile. She was going to launch her own clothing line, which was happening in a shop I had never heard of. I checked the date. It was tonight, and it had a guest list.

#

I waited outside the shop, which had a red carpet, and black balloons were floating at the entrance, and I could hear music, chatter, and laughter. I tapped my feet impatiently, checked the time on my phone, and tucked into my scarf. It was chilly out, but at least it wasn't raining. People strolled past me with shopping bags, some tapping on their phones, not watching where they were going, and some holding hands here and there.

After a twenty-minute wait, I made out a flicking of a cigarette as Jan strolled with ease as if he was in no hurry.

'Where were you? I've been waiting out here for twenty minutes!' I hissed.

'Nice to see you,' he said. 'It was kind of last-minute, and you should thank me for getting you on that list. I had to leave the artist in the middle of a painting. It was unprofessional on my part.'

'I didn't know you could paint,' I commented.

'Not me. I was the model.'

'Oh.'

'It wasn't a nude portrait, in case you were wondering.'

I scoffed. 'I wasn't wondering.'

He was beautifully adorned in jewellery and trinkets and dressed in a red velvet jacket. His black hair rested below his shoulder, an earring dangled on his ear, and he smelt of luxury. I had a feeling he rushed to his apartment to get changed before getting here.

'You know jeans and a t-shirt exist, right?'

'I wouldn't be caught dead in them.'

'It must be exhausting to be you.'

'Shall we, Ms Clarke?'

I let Jan do all the talking with the perky short girl who stood by the shop entrance. With her green hair and a tattoo on her thigh, she ran her polished red finger on the list, then flipped the page looking through the list of names.

'Ah, there you are, Jan and Emily,' she said.

She looked at me, then up at him. We must have made one hell of a couple, him overly elegant and me graceless.

She pulled the red string. 'Have fun! Help yourself to champagne.'

I smiled as we made our way in. A waiter stood with a tray filled with pink champagne.

'Champagne?' Jan asked.

'I'll pass.'

The shop was large with white marble, and there were many people and even photographers.

'I didn't know Apolonia was a household name.'

'In this community, she is.'

'And how do you know her?'

'I had the pleasure of working with her. She's also a talented photographer.'

I scanned the area. 'I'm sure she is.'

I walked past the rails of clothes. I expected them to be black, but there were many colours, ranging from black, grey, blue, pink and red. A beautiful long-sleeved dress caught my eye. It was long with a Spanish blouse. I found the tag and immediately dropped it as my eyes were about to pop out of their sockets.

'Not in your price range?' Jan asked.

'I think my soul just left my body.' I gasped.

He laughed.

Apolonia was talking to a woman in a large hat. Apolonia wore a red dress with nude heels, and her long golden blonde hair reached her waist. Something about her reminded me of Rapunzel; she looked like she belonged in a fairy tale. She saw Jan, and her face lit up. Then she excused herself to the woman with the large hat and walked over.

'Jan!' she screeched, throwing her long arms around him. 'So glad to see you,' she said, giving him pecks on his cheeks. 'So happy you made it. I thought you weren't coming.'

'I changed my mind. How are you, darling? You look stunning as always,' he said.

'Not as stunning as you. I don't know how you do it.'

Her eyes went to me. 'Hi,' she said, extending her hand. 'I'm Apolonia, the creator of this range. Do you see anything you like?'

'Oh, we met, actually,' I said.

Her eyes widened. 'We did? I'm sorry. I meet many people every day. Remind me where?'

'At another event. I was with Sasha.'

Her pretty face turned from cheery to sour. 'Oh yes, you wanted to talk to me about the wedding.'

'Do you have a minute, darling?' Jan said, his voice coated with sugar. 'We need to talk to you.'

'Well, Jan, as you can see, I'm in the middle of something,' she said.

'It's important, and it will only take a few minutes,' he said.

'Oh, what the hell,' she said. 'Might as well get it over and done with.' She passed a look at me. 'Follow me.'

She turned and walked through the crowd as people greeted her. Jan placed the empty glasses of champagne on the passing tray and took another, and I did the same. Promising myself that it would be just that one drink. She walked by the till and opened a door where clothes were stored.

'I'll give you five minutes. Be quick,' she barked.

'Emily and I got in a pickle the night of the wedding,' Jan said.

'Oh, what happened?' she asked.

'Someone drugged us,' he explained.

She crossed her arms under her chest. 'Shouldn't you be telling this to the police?'

'We thought it best if we handled the matter ourselves,' I weighed in. 'We can't remember much of what happened and were wondering if you could shed some light. Maybe you saw something?'

She sighed.

'We wouldn't ask unless it was important,' Jan said.

'I saw you two at the after-party,' she said.

'Did you see Lucien?' I asked.

'Yes, but at the wedding. He wasn't there at the party. Rumour has it he and Cassie had fallen out, and he got upset and left. I don't know what you want me to tell you.

You left the party, and I stayed there with Sasha and Lloyd,' she explained.

'Were you staying at the hotel?' I asked her.

'No, but I stayed until the very end,' she said and looked at Jan. 'I saw you two outside the hotel, heading opposite the club. I don't know where you were going, but you were all over the place.' She cast a sharp glance at me. 'Both of you, I mean, you guys were smashed.'

'Did you see where we went?' Jan asked.

'As I said, in the opposite direction of the club. You were shouting.'

'Did you speak to either of us?' Jan asked.

Apolonia narrowed her eyes at him. 'I tried calling you, and you told me to fuck off.'

Jan grimaced. 'Oh, how rude of me.'

'Yes,' Apolonia agreed. 'It was rude.'

'If you had seen us,' I said, 'and you saw we were out of it, why didn't you help us? Or call for help?'

This question threw her. She opened her mouth to speak, but there was a knock, and the door opened. A woman popped her head in. 'We need your help.'

Apolonia looked at us. 'I really need to go. It was nice of you to come.'

This registered with Jan. 'Hope you solve your mystery,' she told him, giving him pecks on the cheek.

We followed her out of the storage room back into the loud music and chatter. Apolonia walked up to a couple with her arms outstretched. Apolonia had seen us outside the hotel, begging the question, where was Yovanna? Was she with her?

Chapter Twenty-Nine

Who was the woman Anna mentioned? Where was Yovanna? And did Lucien really leave the hotel? What else did Cassie know? Did someone come to Jan's room? I reached for the key and played around with it in my hand. Was this the same person who sent me the note?

I walked towards the window and looked out. It was drizzling out, and lightning sounded in the distance. I returned to work, and from time to time, I stopped and stared at the key, trying to think of what it might open and who had left it. I went to Facebook, and Lucien had reactivated his accounts, even his fan page. Where could he be? Was he at Cassie's? Sasha's? Jan's? No, those were the last places he'd be.

I returned to work, and when I looked up, it was dark out. I stood, stretched, made a pot of noodles and toast for dinner and poured myself a generous glass of wine. I returned to my desk and ate my unsatisfying dinner, watching funny cat videos on YouTube.

I filled myself with another glass of wine and lay in the bath holding the key in my hand, making my hands clammy from pressing it against my palms so hard. I closed my eyes and thought of that pretty yellow door, but what was behind that door wasn't so pretty. Olivia had turned the place around and given it life. My eyes snapped open, and I was filled with the sense of knowing what door that key opened and who had left it there for me.

#

Most of the houses were dark as the Uber driver pulled onto my old street. I got out of the car and looked at the yellow door that shone through the orange lights. The house was in darkness. Olivia wasn't there, but someone else was. I glanced at Agnes's house, and the upstairs light was on. Was she in there looking out? Could she see me? I stalked towards the yellow door that seemed to have grown three sizes bigger and put the key in the lock. I shut my eyes, fearing an alarm would go off and disturb the quiet street. There was a click, but no alarm sounded.

The hallway was dark, but the moonlight offered me enough guidance to manoeuvre around the rooms and avoid breaking something. I walked through the living room and emerged into the kitchen. I could distinctly make out someone sitting behind the table.

'Lucien?' I whispered.

'You worked it out, finally,' he said.

I located the switch, and an explosion of light came on. Lucien shut his eyes, annoyed by this move. I stood by the entrance, staring at him. He opened his eyes, and we took each other in.

He wore a grey tunic and beige linen trousers tucked inside black boots with thick rubber soles. He wore lots of jewellery, and a long green scarf was wrapped around his long delicate neck. His white blonde hair was long, reaching his waist, and two thin braids were dangling on his shoulders. Despite the baffling outfit, he looked absolutely gorgeous. But Lucien could smear himself with shit, and he'd pull it off. Some people were just born blessed.

'You could have asked me to ring the bell like a normal person instead of leaving me a key,' I said.

'It's better this way,' he said.

'What is wrong with you? Why are you being so… odd?'

There was a bottle of red wine on the table and a glass.

'I had to get away.'

'You fucked off to Berlin doing God knows what and left everyone here worried and angry. Not to mention that the police were looking for you.'

'And I wish I'd stayed there,' he said. 'I'm so over this drama.'

I took a step closer. 'I assume the police informed you about what happened.'

'Yes, they did.'

'And?'

'Bad shit keeps happening. I can't take it.'

'Yes, it's called life. You can't run away from that.'

'No, but I can start over.'

'In Berlin?'

He stared at me.

I rubbed my forehead. 'What's in Berlin that you had to leave a wedding and your friend who had just lost her husband?'

'I didn't know about that. I had already landed when Lloyd died,' he said.

'Just stop with the mystery for once and tell me,' I snapped.

'I went to find my biological father.'

He went to find his father in Berlin? Was his father living there? Was his father German? He could have informed someone he was going, at least. I thought he said he didn't want to know who his real father was, but I guess his curiosity got the better of him.

I stared at him, shocked, trying to find my voice. I cleared my throat and tried again.

'I thought you said you didn't want to know who he was,' I said.

'I changed my mind. I asked my mum about him. I have every right to know who he is.'

'Of course,' I agreed. 'But you could have at least told someone.'

'Mum knew, but I told her not to tell anyone.'

'You didn't even tell Henry?'

He peered at me. 'Why? It would only upset him. I have upset many people as it is.'

He cast me a guilty look, then broke eye contact. I thought of the letters that Henry had sent.

'Did you find him, your father?' I asked.

'Yes, he's dead.'

The way he said *dead* with no emotion. Not even a hint of sadness, just detachment.

'He's dead?'

'Yes. Dead.'

To go through that trouble, to be filled with hope, with only disappointment awaiting you.

I moved the chair, which scraped loudly against the floor, and sat across from him. 'I'm so sorry, that's awful.'

'It's all right,' he said, not looking at me but focusing on something on the floor. 'I'm not upset or anything.'

'You're not?' I asked.

His eyes went up to me. 'I never knew him. How could I be upset? Henry is my father. He was just someone that brought me to this existence.'

'How did he die?' I asked.

'He's been dead for five years. Cancer.'

'I see. So, he's German, your father?'

He glared at me. 'Yes, it seemed he met Mum while staying here for work.'

'What did he do?'

'He was a photographer.'

I smiled. 'So the talent comes from him.'

'No,' he said. 'The talent comes from *me*. I worked hard for it. What about you, Emily? What were you up to? Did you miss me?'

'Yes, I missed you.'

He lowered his eyes, hiding them behind long eyelashes. 'And yet you…'

He cleared his throat and reached for the glass of wine.

'Lucien, you and me, we're complicated,' I began. 'But in the hospital, when you told me you were through with fucking around, you didn't mean it, did you?'

He looked at me sharply. 'Yes, I did. Why would I need to fuck around when I have everything I need?'

'But if you want to change, you do it for yourself, not for someone else.'

He stood. 'I took a fucking bullet for you. Tell me, who else can say that to you, Emily? What more do you want? I would die for you. I would kill for you.'

'Don't say those things.'

He placed his hands on the table and leaned forward. 'Why not?'

I leaned back in the chair. 'Did you leave the hotel at midnight?'

He moved away and leaned against the kitchen counter. 'Yes, Cassie and I had a fight.'

'She said. According to her, you were in a bad mood.'

He glared at me. 'You spoke to Cassie?'

'Yes, you left me no choice. I was worried.'

'Oh, I bet you were,' he said bitterly.

'Why are you being like this?'

'Like what?'

'Bitter and angry. You have people who love and care for you.'

'That's because I am bitter and angry.'

I sighed. 'I am affected by this as much as you are.'

'But your parents are not in prison, Emily. That fucks you up. You weren't shot either.'

'Is that what we've come to, Lucien? Scoring points? Really?'

'I left the wedding… and it was the other way around. Cassie started the fight, not me. And I had the flight booked already.'

That meant Cassie was lying.

'Why are you asking me these questions? Did something happen to you?' he asked.

'Yes, something happened, not just to me, but Jan too.'

'Jan?'

'Yes, remember him? Your friend who refused to leave your bedside when you were in the hospital?'

'He's like a brother to me.'

This hangs in the air, polluted. Like a brother to him. And if Lucien finds out that I had sex with him, that brotherhood would be over, and I'd be responsible for it.

'What happened?' he insisted.

'We were drugged.'

'What? Seriously? Who would do that? Why?'

'That's what we're trying to find out.'

'We?'

'Jan and I.'

'I didn't know you and Jan had become this close.'

There was an edge to his voice.

'At the hospital we—'

He lifted his hand. 'Never mind… I don't care.'

'I think whoever drugged us is connected to Lloyd's...
fall.'

'He didn't fall. Someone pushed him,' he corrected me.

'And you saw nothing unusual that night?'

'No, it was a wedding. There were lots of people.'

'But whoever killed Lloyd was a guest at that wedding.
Lloyd was your friend, wasn't he? There are photos on
social media to prove that. Was he in some sort of trouble?
I don't know. Maybe he owed money to someone or
crossed someone. Sasha said he didn't, but he could have
kept it from her.'

'I don't know. We were friends, but I wasn't in bed with
him,' he snapped.

Yet he slept with both men and women. It wouldn't
surprise me if he blurted out that he had slept with Lloyd
too. And I was slowly being sucked into this orbit of sexual
explorations, doing messed up shit like having sex with Jan.
I was drunk, but it didn't excuse my behaviour. And I
should have eased with the drinking when I promised
myself I would. Now Sasha had kissed me on the lips,
which came out of nowhere, and my relationship with her
was platonic. Maybe that was how it was in their circle.
Everyone kissed whoever they liked and slept with who
they wanted because why not? They were a bunch of

stunning people who wore lots of black and liked to have fun, and trouble seemed to follow them everywhere.

'So, you don't know who might have drugged us?' I asked.

He narrowed his eyes at me. 'What are you suggesting, Emily, that I snuck back in the hotel and drugged you and Jan with ecstasy? Why would I do that?'

I stared at him, alarmed. 'How do you know it was ecstasy?'

'I don't. I'm just guessing. It's a common drug used to spike people's drinks.'

'You seem quite knowledgeable on the subject.'

'It happened to me once,' he confessed.

'What? You got drugged without your consent?'

'Well… sort of….'

'What did you do?'

'Nothing. I woke up in a random bed with a boy and a girl.'

'You slept with them?'

His silence was enough to tell me that he did.

I could gape at him. His reasoning was too confusing to me. He sauntered around the table, graceful as a cat. The moonlight glowed behind him, and I watched him coming closer until he stood by my chair and took my hand gently.

His touch was cold, and my body had a life of its own as it snapped me up on my feet.

As we stood in the quiet in his old house, which was now renovated beyond recognition, I asked myself, what did he see? This twenty-seven-year-old specimen surrounded himself with the most beautiful people, and then there was me; I had been described as pretty and beautiful too, but I was nothing near the level of these people. What did he see? Why me? He ran his fingers through my hair as my heart jumped and kicked into my chest. My breath rose and fell, and the walls were crashing down on me. My hands were shaking. My whole body was convulsing, making my head want to explode.

Chapter Thirty

The night of Sasha's wedding...

'Would you like to dance?' Jan asked.

By that time, the alcohol buzzed in my system, and a rush of joy pulsed through me. When had I last had this much fun? Not in this past year and a half. It seemed like a lifetime ago.

'No,' I replied.

Lady Gaga was in full swing now, and he gave me a playful grin and looked away, making a face pretending to be hurt. Then he smiled again, and I smiled too. *Oh, what the hell,* I thought. *I deserve this, this fun. I earned it. To hell with it all. I have a right to it, this fun. This happiness I'm feeling.*

I stumbled onto the dancefloor, not giving a damn who was watching. I was a single woman, and I could do whatever pleased me. So, I danced, drank, and laughed. The laughter was the genuine kind that came from the belly, and I couldn't remember the last time I had laughed like that. Jan pulled me to him, and my hand rested on his chest as he gazed down at me. *So beautiful,* I thought, *so utterly gorgeous.* A god among gods. There was a look in his eyes that I recognised—desire, and it was there something was decided between us. It was silent but understood. Without saying a word, he took my hand and led me out of the dance floor, taking me away from that noise in the chilly air of the night.

'Jan,' I said, giggling as we walked.

'Yes?'

'Where are we going?'

'To a magic carpet ride,' he said.

We both bubbled into uncontrollable laughter. I was making pig-like snorts, and he laughed even harder. We walked into the hotel, joking, and talking about things that weren't worth remembering and then, out of the blue, he picked me up and spun me around until I was dizzy. My head rolled as the lift pinged, and he took me inside with me still wrapped around him, and we crashed to the wall, kissing, our hands all over each other. I didn't think of anything. My mind was empty. There wasn't a single thought in there. There was, at last, silence. He put me down when the lift announced we'd arrived at his floor, and we didn't speak as he fumbled in his pockets for the card.

We threw ourselves into one another and went inside as he slammed the door behind us, and I held him like a climbing, coiling vine invading every part of him.

#

We collapsed on the bed, panting, our cheeks raw. I just lay there, drunk and tired.

'That was a crazy ride.' He laughed. 'I thought we were going to break the bed.'

'Ahh,' I said.

He placed his hand on my crotch. 'Heaven.'

'Oh! Oh! Oh, God,' I cried.

He sniggered. 'This was amazing.'

He sat up from the bed, zipped his trousers, walked around the bed, and picked something nude and silky. It took me a while to realise what they were.

'Give me those!' I protested.

He smiled but ignored me as he went to the dressing table and reached for the Post-it notes. His back was to mine, and I couldn't see what he was doing. He threw my underwear in the basket along with his necklace and stuck the Post-it on the basket. On the Post-it were two tiny hearts. The reason he had done this was beyond me. Just being drunk and foolish.

His blue eyes flickered to mine, smirking. He leaned against the dressing table and rolled a cigarette. He smoked while I lay there, trying to process it all. Then he stood and came to the bed, staring down at me.

'Jan, what are we doing?' I asked.

His mouth tasted of cigarettes and champagne.

'For once, don't think, just do... enjoy the moment,' he whispered and licked my lips.

He entered me again. I let out a grunt, and everything melted away.

#

It dawned on me what we had done. How wrong it was. That we shouldn't have done this in the first place. I couldn't believe that I could do such a thing and behave this way. I was a grown woman, not a teenage girl who got caught up in her lust for a gorgeous man that gave her attention. What was wrong with me? How could I do this? This time, I went too far. Despite what I felt, I didn't voice any of it.

'Get dressed, Emily. The party is not over yet,' Jan announced.

'But—'

'We sleep when we're dead.'

I thought nothing of this and put my dress back on, forgetting about the underwear. We walked down the corridor, and his card dropped on the floor; I picked it up, placed it in my bag, and followed Jan to the bar. We ordered two glasses of white wine, and Cassie came over.

She might have been in the bar's corner, and we didn't see her.

'You still here?' Jan asked.

'Yeah, Lucien fucked off, and I'm bored,' she said.

Jan didn't ask her to join us, but she took it upon herself to sit beside Jan and order a pint. They talked for a while, unsure about what. I excused myself to go to the bathroom. I was feeling drowsy, but I didn't vomit. I caught myself in the mirror when I came out of the stall. My hair was a tangled mess, and my make-up was slightly smudged. *Too far*, I thought, *this had gone too far*. I ripped the paper from the machine and wiped the smudges off my eyes. My lips were puffy, but I didn't apply any lipstick. I left the bathroom, and Jan was on his way to the men's room.

'You okay?' he asked.

I must have said I was okay and gone back to the bar. Cassie was speaking to the bartender and looked at me. I returned to my stool, thinking I should call it a night. Jan came back, and Cassie said she was going to go.

We finished our drink, and we walked to the hotel lobby. Lloyd walked in with a woman, not Sasha. This one had long black hair and was wearing a silky black dress. Yovanna. No, that wasn't right. That made no sense. Why would Lloyd walk into the hotel with Yovanna, not with

Sasha? What was going on? I had to be mistaken. Where was Sasha?

Jan looked up and said something I couldn't seem to recall. The memory was still fuzzy. Lloyd's face paled, and he walked out of the hotel. Jan ran after him, and a strange sensation waved all over my body. A mix of nausea and muscles spasming. I opened my mouth to call out something, maybe for Jan to wait.

I was out in the hotel into the night barefooted, unsure how my shoes were taken off. Maybe in my drunken haze, I left them in my room, and neither Jan nor the hotel staff had noticed. I ambled towards the street, and there was shouting. Apolonia came from behind me, and her shoulder crashed into mine. Between the confusion and panic rising through my body of not knowing what was happening, I fell to the pavement. She didn't stop nor look back but went charging after Jan, Lloyd and Yovanna. With difficulty, I got back up and found my way back to the hotel. Nausea hit me harder now, and everything around me spun. Heat rushed into my body as my heart hammered against my chest. I located the lift and somehow found a way into the room, and everything disintegrated into nothingness.

Chapter Thirty-One

I moved away from Lucien as if his grip would torch me to flames.

'What's wrong?' he asked.

'I need to…'

'Emily!'

I staggered out of the living room, heaving. My mouth was dry as sandpaper, and my heart rolled on my rib cage. My hands were shaking, and the room was spinning. Lucien led me to the sofa and made me sit down.

'Easy, you're having a panic attack. Take deep breaths,' he instructed.

He sat with me as I breathed in and out, in and out. I did that for a while, and the slamming of my heart eased, and everything turned calm again. Lucien stood and went to the kitchen. I heard him open a cupboard and return with a glass of water. I took a sip of water and stared at the carpet.

'What happened?' he asked, concerned. 'What triggered this panic attack?'

I looked at him. 'I just remembered something.'

'What? What did you remember?'

'I…'

'Is it about the wedding? Jesus, Emily. What the hell happened that made you like this? Do you want me to call you a doctor?'

'No, I'm fine.'

He didn't look convinced. 'Maybe I should take you to the hospital.'

'No!' I protested.

'Have you had them before? The panic attacks, I mean?'

I shook my head, placed the glass on the coffee table, and stood. Lucien stood as well, reaching for me, but I shook him off.

'I need to go.'

'Wait.'

I ambled to the front door. 'I need to be alone and think.'

I could hear his footsteps stomping behind me. 'Emily, you're in no cond—'

'Just back off!' I shouted, shutting the door behind me.

#

Cassie and Apolonia had lied to Jan and me to our faces. Cassie didn't leave the wedding after Lucien had left. She might have been at the bar when Jan and I walked to the hotel, and she followed us. Her lingering in the corridor gave me the creeps, and she was the one that had drugged our drinks. There was no question about it. She had plenty of time. Between me in the bathroom and Jan going there a few minutes after, she could have slipped the pills into our glasses. She might have picked a random conversation with the bartender to distract her. But why? Was she jealous? Did she have a crush on Jan? Did she get mad seeing me with him? But she was with Lucien. He introduced her as his girlfriend to me but then didn't tell Olivia he had a woman in his life. That meant he said that to spite me, to make me jealous or to annoy me. Immature and childish on his part. Was there someone who was involved with Lucien that wasn't remotely fucked up? First his mother, then Travis, now Cassie too? He surely attracted them.

Then there was Apolonia and Yovanna. Where did they fit in all of this? What was their business with Lloyd? Why would a newlywed man choose to leave his own party to go to a hotel with a woman who wasn't his wife? Where was Sasha all this time? I suppose she was distracted by friends and family, and it was easy for him and Yovanna to slip past without anyone noticing. But why? What was so important? Was Lloyd seeing her behind Sasha's back? Or maybe Sasha knew about it with their liberal way of thinking. This was a woman who slept with Jan over a disagreement she had with Lloyd. Did Sasha know that Lloyd had left the party with Yovanna?

Cassie had spiked our drinks, and something was going on between Yovanna and Lloyd. And there was Apolonia, who pushed me and went after them. Why did she do that? Did she have a secret grudge against me that I wasn't aware of? She pushed me to stop me from going after Jan and Lloyd. What didn't she want me to see? What was she hiding?

#

Anna was already at Starbucks, which was located three doors down from her office. I had called her, asking her desperately to meet up. I could have done it on Facebook, but it was better to meet in person. She was eating a sandwich when I walked in, and a large cappuccino mug was on the table.

'You look like hell,' she said.

'That's because I feel like hell.'

She stopped chewing. 'What's wrong?'

'Lucien is back,' I announced.

'Oh no. You spoke to him?'

'Yes.'

'Where did he go?'

'To Berlin.'

'Beside The Berghain nightclub, what was so important that he had to go there?'

'His biological father.'

'Oh,' she said.

'And did he find him? His father?'

'Yes, he died five years ago. Cancer.'

'Oh my God, that is awful, the poor sod. He must be devastated,' Anna cried.

'That's the strange thing,' I said. 'He's not.'

Anna's eyes widened. 'He's not upset? To go all the way there to find out his father had been dead for ages? Did his mother not know he'd passed?'

I shook my head. 'I don't know, but she knew he went to Berlin.'

Anna blinked. 'And she didn't tell anyone?'

'Nope, Lucien told her not to.'

'He didn't even inform Henry?'

An image of unopened letters came to me, all from Henry pleading for what? To know why Lucien wasn't visiting him? Why handwritten letters, not emails? The prison might have computers.

'No,' I said. 'He didn't tell Henry.'

'What are you going to do now?' she asked.

'There is something I have to show you,' I said, reaching for the phone and finding a photo of Yovanna and showing it to Anna.

'Is this the woman who came to speak to Lloyd?'

Anna squinted at the screen. 'Yes, that's her.'

'Are you sure this was her?' I asked.

'Yes, it was her. Who is she?'

'Someone connected to our mutual friends.'

Chapter Thirty-Two

A peal of thunder rolled as I stood by the window. I hardly got any work done these past few days, and I didn't want to think of my inbox full of unread emails with clients demanding this and that. I hadn't told anyone yet about gaining my memory back from that night. Not Jan or Anna. I should tell Jan, though. He had every right to know, but I didn't want to see him.

My phone pinged, and I knew who it was. Lucien hadn't stopped texting or calling since I had left Olivia's house. I shook my head with disapproval. Did this guy think he could do whatever he wanted because of his appearance? He couldn't be reached for weeks, and now that he was back, he expected what? For me to jump when he called? *Fuck him*, I thought. *Fuck them all*. I had behaved disgustingly, like a lustful teenage girl who couldn't handle her drink. I had behaved that way since I'd met and befriended the strange and beautiful blond living in the house across the street with its yellow door and his odd parents. It felt like I was living a stolen life that wasn't truly mine. I sat on the sofa, placed my hand over my head, and silently screamed. *When was this going to end? When is it going to go away? All of it.*

I wasn't okay. I was far from okay, and I should pick up the phone and call the number of that therapist that Sasha had recommended.

The buzzer made me jump. I stood and saw Lucien on the screen. Rolling my eyes, I let him in. I might as well face him, or he would keep bugging me. I opened the door and left it ajar as I turned, facing the window. The rain had stopped now, and I could hear the swoosh of tyres from outside. Not once had Lucien been here in this flat. There was no reason for him to be here. Now, he was on his way up here to invade my space. *I shouldn't have let him in,* I thought. I should have left him outside while I stayed here, not making a sound, pretending I didn't exist.

He pushed the door open, and there he stood, all six feet of him dressed in the same outfit as the other night.

'What is wrong with you?' he demanded.

'What is wrong with me?' I asked.

'Yeah, you screamed at me, and you left,' he said, dismayed.

I stomped to the kitchen. 'It's more than you deserve.'

He followed me to the kitchen, his cologne wafting in the air. Great, his cologne would linger in my apartment. I reached for a glass of wine.

'What is going on, Emily?' he barked.

Rage ignited through my veins, and I dropped the wine glass to the floor. 'I had sex with Jan!'

The silence was so defined, so still, you could hear a pin drop. He stood there staring at me, his eyes wide. His expression was something I couldn't read. It wasn't angry. Not hurt. Not disappointed. There was no hint of betrayal there, either. Just icy.

'Well, for someone who always made judgements on how we do things and live our lives and how immoral we are, you fit quite well in our circle.'

His tone reeked of sarcasm.

'Don't,' I said. 'Don't patronise me. I feel like shit. I haven't slept in weeks.'

He raised his eyebrows. 'Why? Because you fucked my friend, who you clearly like?'

I stared at him, aghast.

'You made it quite obvious, making remarks about how gorgeous he is. Jan has always been a looker. The best-looking one out of the bunch,' he added.

I scoffed and walked past him. 'As if you're not? *Please,* you're a fucking messiah.'

'So you're saying I deserve everything I got because of the way I look? That I'm being punished for it?' he said incredulously.

'That is not what I meant. Just leave, Lucien. Since you people walked into my life, there has been nothing but ruin,' I said in distress.

'Oh, I see, so I'm Helen of Troy, is that it? I bring nothing but chaos and pestilence. As if I bought this upon you. This is not *my* fault. None of this is. And,' he said, walking closer to me, his face inches from mine, 'it doesn't make it okay to sleep with my friend.'

I went to the sofa. 'Oh, please, you sleep with everyone!'

'I never hid who I was, unlike you,' he said, looking at me up and down in disdain. 'Miss Perfect.'

I turned to him. 'Miss Perfect? Me? Look at me, Lucien. I'm falling apart. I'm all over the place. My life was fine before I moved into that forsaken house and befriended you and your insane mother.'

'Don't talk like that about my mum.'

'Oh, shut up, just shut up!'

'You fucked him at the wedding, did you?' he asked, ignoring my protest.

I focused on the wall. 'Yes.'

'I knew it.'

I gaped at him. 'Knew what? You barely acknowledged me at the wedding. You looked and spoke to me as if I were a piece of gum stuck at the bottom of your shoe!'

'I was hurt. What do you expect? You rejected me,' he argued.

'I told you we would see. I didn't give you a definite answer, but your ego just couldn't handle it. I needed time. Do you think that was easy for me?'

'And you just couldn't wait to rush into Jan's arms,' he said.

'Oh, stop it. You are young and crazy!'

'Because Jan is not young and crazy?' he reasoned.

'Look, I'm sorry. I'm a terrible person and clearly am a bitch, but I don't want you to stop being friends with him because of this.'

'Stop being friends with Jan? Are you insane?' he snapped. 'He's like a brother to me. Do you think I'd stop being friends with him because of *you*? Is that what you think? We have a stronger bond than to end a friendship over something so petty.'

'Then why are you being like this?' I asked.

'I'm not happy about it, and it's the hypocrisy that bothers me.'

'Who are you calling a hypocrite?' I retorted.

'You are, Emily. *You.* Always going on about making up my mind. I'm too promiscuous. Blah, blah, blah. You are not so different from us, after all.'

'I am nothing like you and your lot! Once, I had too much to drink and got carried away. *Just once.* That one time. I was just having fun! I didn't mean for anything like this to happen.'

He narrowed his eyes at me. 'And that is what we do, Emily. We have fun, and we both know you like the bottle too much. It wasn't that one time you had too much to drink now, was it?'

'I will not stand here and be judged like this by an immature, selfish little boy!'

'An immature, selfish little boy, huh? Is that all you have, Emily? It's the *truth.* You do have a problem.'

'Oh, fuck off, just fuck off.'

'Go to hell, you fucking scrubber!' he shouted, stomping to the front door and slamming it so hard that I thought the door was going to break. And then, into the silence came a resounding *bang! Bang! Bang!* I jumped. My downstairs neighbour was pounding on the ceiling with a broom handle, telling me to keep the noise down. I stared at the door; it wasn't broken, but I was.

Chapter Thirty-Three

I spent my days locked in my apartment with the windows closed, burying myself at work and in misery. I cleaned my apartment until it was spotless, threw all the wine bottles in the bin, and took the bags out to be collected. I watched porn for a reason that was beyond me, then became disgusted with myself. I switched off my laptop, deleted the history from my browser to remove the evidence of my shame, and went to bed and tried to get some sleep. I had a nightmare about Sylvain, Amanda and Ed climbing out of the well with their bodies decomposing and bugs coming out from where their eyes used to be and from their mouths.

I woke up sweating and confused, then lay on the sweat-soaked pillow, thinking of Ed. I thought of him a lot, especially that afternoon when he came to my house after I caught him cheating and hitting me. That was when it all began. My gratitude for the bloke across the street who saw the whole thing from his bedroom window and took it upon himself to intervene. If only I didn't answer the door that day, if only Lucien didn't interfere, it wouldn't have piqued my curiosity about him. I wouldn't be in this mess in the first place. I would be just Emily Clarke, a digital marketer working from home to earn a living who was up for a good laugh. An ordinary woman living her life.

I watched the sun rising from beneath the curtains. Then, with an effort, I got out of bed, made a strong coffee and checked my emails while drinking it. Olivia sent me an email with a picture. Her husband might have taken the picture as she posed with her hands on her hips with the Griffith Observatory behind her. I smiled and sent her a reply, hoping she was having fun. I wanted to add that I spoke to Lucien but then deleted it. I didn't want to spoil her holiday, and I was sure he would get in touch.

I went to Facebook, and I had a notification that I was invited to an event Jan would host. A small gathering at his apartment. I exited the event page with a shaking head and checked my single message, assuming it was from Lucien to pass some hateful remarks about my life choices. Thinking no good was going to come out of this, I clicked on it, but it was Jan.

Come to this party. Yovanna is going to be there. Xxx.

The gathering was two days from now, which made me think he'd planned this and forgot to invite me, or it was a last-minute thing. I suspected it was the latter. He found out something. Did he remember too? I almost called him until I realised it might still be too early for him.

I dressed in jeans and a jumper and took the tube. I marched to the street, looking at the yellow door. I kept walking and rang Agnes's bell, and a man I had never seen before opened the door.

'Yes?' he asked.

He was in his forties, with large hazel eyes and black hair. He was dressed in a black polo shirt and black jeans. He had to be her son, and I should have called rather than showing up unannounced.

'Good morning, I'm Emily. Is Agnes in? I'm her old neighbour.'

He looked over his shoulder, then stepped outside, shutting the door behind him.

'I'm Stephen, her son. I'm afraid there has been an incident.'

My heart missed a beat for that tiny moment as the colour drained from my face. It was then I noticed his eyes were red from crying.

'What happened?' I asked with a shaking voice.

'She had a stroke. She's at the hospital—'

Oh no, oh no, no, no, no. I couldn't handle more bad news. Poor Agnes Parker might have been noisy to the point of being annoying, but she was a nice old lady.

'Can I see her?'

'I'm afraid she is not stable at the moment.'

I gasped. 'I'm so sorry. I... God, poor Agnes. Can you keep me updated on her condition?'

'Um... sure, of course. She has an address book. Will I find you in there?'

'Yes, she called me several times.'

He nodded, turned and shut the door, leaving me staring at Agnes's front door.

#

I turned, crossed the road toward the yellow door, and rang the bell. As I waited, I thought of Agnes. I only saw her a few days ago, and I refused her offer of tea. I thought of her hopeful eyes, and this thought morphed into regret. I should have accepted her offer. Now there was a possibility that—Lucien answered the door, rubbing his eyes with the back of his hand.

'I'm sorry,' I said. 'I made a mess out of everything... I'm...' I puffed. 'Can we talk?'

Without saying a word, he turned, leaving me to deal with the front door.

He stomped to the kitchen, and I followed him. He put on the kettle and fingered his hair, looking deep in thought.

'Is this a good idea? You staying here?' I asked.

He looked at me sharply. 'I used to live here, Emily, and now it looks like a different house either way with all of this…' He looked with disapproval around the kitchen. 'Stuff.'

'Shouldn't you get a place of your own instead of hopping about from one place to another?'

'I'll figure out something.'

'Have you spoken to Cassie?'

He snorted. 'She hates me.'

'That's a little extreme.'

'She does for now… until she loves me again. It's like a game we play.'

'She's the one who drugged us. That is why I had a panic attack the night I came here. It all came back to me. She did it.'

Lucien passed me a sardonic look. 'Why would Cassie do that?'

'I don't know. Do you?'

'Me? Yeah, she told me she planned to drug you and Jan,' Lucien said sarcastically. 'Cassie didn't even know you were invited to the wedding.'

'Wait,' I said, taking a step closer to him. 'She didn't know?'

He made the coffees. 'No.'

'But she knew Jan would be there?' I asked.

Lucien stirred the coffees. 'Without a doubt.'

'So, she planned to drug Jan?'

'How can you be sure it's her? Maybe you're mistaken.'

'She followed us.'

'Where?'

'To…' I trailed off.

He looked at me. 'Don't be coy now, Emily. She followed you and Jan to his hotel room and heard him fucking you.'

I looked away. 'You have a way with words.'

Lucien placed a mug of coffee on the table. 'I'm stating basic facts here.'

'You're bitter, and you hate me. I'm so sorry I…' I trailed off and sniffed.

He sat on the chair and probed his socked feet on the kitchen table. 'You're the last person in this world I would hate, and I'm sorry for calling you a scrubber. That was… nasty.'

I sat across from him. 'Have you spoken to—'

'Jan, yes. Last night…'

I looked at him, worried. 'We are still friends, don't worry. We will remain friends. *Always*. It was a weapon I wanted to use against you… to hurt you for the… rejection.'

We sipped our coffees, letting the silence settle between us.

'So, Cassie and Jan,' he said, breaking the silence.

'Why would she drug Jan? Does she have a grudge against him?'

Lucien took a sip of coffee, pondering on this. 'She used to have a massive crush on Jan. *Huge*. Each time he turned up, her eyes turned into hearts.'

I stared at him. 'And did he reciprocate her feelings?'

Lucien shrugged. 'He was playful, cheeky and flirted with her. But for her... it morphed into an obsession.'

'Excuse me for being blunt, but did he sleep with her?'

'I don't know... he didn't tell me anything, and it's not like Jan is going to tell me each detailed sexual encounter he has with someone. She said nothing either.'

I rubbed my forehead. Friends sleeping with each other—it was so strange to me. They were either your friend or they weren't, but who was I to judge?

'When was this?' I asked.

He looked up at the ceiling, thinking. 'About two years ago. I often caught her staring at Jan in that dreamy way that people do. Sometimes I felt sorry for her.'

'Why?'

'Because it got pathetic.'

'And then?'

'Then nothing. She moved on, and one night, we were at a party, and we hooked up.'

'And when did you become an item?' I asked.

'We were never an item, Emily. I was living with her, but we weren't exclusive. After Travis…' He sighed. 'I won't allow someone in like that ever again.'

Yet he wanted to be with me. He trusted me. He loved me.

'I said that at the wedding to make you… I don't know… jealous. I'm pathetic,' he said.

'You are not pathetic,' I said.

He smiled.

'So that is why you never told Olivia about her?' I asked.

'I have no reason to tell Olivia anything. Did you tell her?'

'Um… I had to…'

He nodded.

Cassie was obsessed with Jan, and then she hooked up with Lucien. Then a realisation donned on me.

I looked at Lucien. 'Do you think she was using you to make everyone think she moved on when she wasn't over Jan?'

He waved his hand as if to dismiss this as ridiculous. 'Nah.'

Was it ridiculous? No, it wasn't, because the truth was in front of me. Cassie was never into Lucien. Maybe she was, but not as much as she was into Jan, but Lucien was the spare wheel she could use. Cassie always wanted the other one, Jan. With his sublime elegance and gorgeousness, he made both Venus and Mars jealous, but he wanted nothing to do with her. Or, knowing Jan, he had hooked up with her to amuse himself, maybe more than once for some good old fun, but then he got bored or wasn't interested anymore and moved on to someone new and exciting. Meanwhile, Cassie got her hopes up and couldn't handle the rejection. I was only assuming here. I didn't know the facts, but I could bet money on it.

Let's presume Cassie kept pining for Jan, hoping and waiting for that perfect moment, and then came the wedding. She and Lucien had a fight. He stormed out of the wedding and left her there. Jan didn't bring a date with him, and she thought this was her chance to hook up with him, but I ruined it for her when I encountered Jan in the bar after I couldn't find Anna anywhere.

Cassie saw us at the after-party, talking and dancing. Feeling left out and hugely disappointed, she went back to the hotel bar to drown her sorrows. She saw us coming into the hotel together drunk, laughing, and making total fools of ourselves, and she suspected where this would go. It was where it usually went when a man and a woman had a little too much to drink and were having a great time. She had to be sure that her suspicions were indeed correct. Cassie went upstairs to the rooms, and she either saw us go in or heard us.

Cassie knew who I was. She must have thought I already had the blond bombshell; now I was going after Jan? She must have been *furious*. Who was I to step in and wreck it all for her? Wasn't Lucien enough? Now I had to go and shag his friend too? Why should I have them both? I was nothing more than an old cow. She was beautiful, curvaceous, and young.

After we ran into her in the bar, Cassie said she was going to her room. We unexpectedly ran into Lloyd, who was accompanied by Yovanna rather than his wife. Lloyd left the hotel, and Jan went after him. What happened afterwards? I made it to the room since I had the key card in my bag, but Jan said he woke up on the pavement.

Cassie got her revenge by drugging us both to get a kick out of it. This all leads to one thing—she had the drugs ready. She brought them with her to the hotel. Meaning this was planned beforehand. If things didn't go as she hoped with Jan, the drugs were her second option. Cassie made it her business to spend the rest of the evening with Jan. She wanted him so badly that she was prepared to drug him if necessary.

Did Cassie make it to her room after the deed was done? Or did she linger somewhere in the dark, biding her time? Did she do something to Jan while he was out? Was she the one that sent Jan and me the underwear and the note with the condom to mess with our heads?

I thought of that photo in Sasha's apartment, of the whole group, and Cassie was at the back looking at Sasha's head. I quickly rummaged through my bag, took out my phone and searched for the photo. Lucien, in the meantime, was watching me with his eyebrows furrowed, probably wondering what I was up to. I found the photo and stared at it, Cassie was at the back and Sasha and Jan were next to one another. My eyes went to Cassie. I got it all wrong. It wasn't Sasha who Cassie was glaring at—it was Jan.

Chapter Thirty-Four

'My God,' I said after the realisation dawned on me.

'What?' Lucien asked.

'Jesus Christ,' I said.

'Emily, you're acting insane. What's wrong?' Lucien asked.

I looked at him. 'She actually did it.'

The confusion on his face was defining. 'What? Did what? Who?'

'Cassie, you idiot.'

'Cassie?'

'Yes, Cassie. She planned it all along.'

'Planned what? You're not making any sense.'

'Cassie was using you to make you all think she was over Jan, but in reality, she wasn't. You were in a bad mood that day.'

'I was a little pissed off, yes, then out of nowhere, she started arguing with me over nothing, and I left.'

'So it was planned…' I confirmed.

'What are you on about?'

'Cassie planned it all, Lucien. She wanted you out of there, knowing that Jan did not bring a date with him. She might have known you had the ticket to Berlin booked. She knew you were going to leave.'

'How could she?'

'She checked your email, maybe?'

'Fuck.'

'She knew you had a flight to catch and set her plan into motion, only I stepped in innocently. She had been watching us all night. Following us then when we went down to the bar afterwards... she showed up out of nowhere, and we left her alone at some point to go to the loo, and that was when she did it.'

He removed his feet from the table and leaned forward. 'You're telling me my friend that I've known for years is so in love with Jan that she... what?'

'She brought the drugs to the hotel as a backup plan in case he didn't accept her... advances.'

'She put a roofie in his drink? Come on!'

'What if that's what she did? What if it's true? Jan and I woke up without remembering what had happened after leaving the hotel. After we had that glass of wine in that bar.'

'That's bonkers.'

'Jan suspects that something like this could have happened. It could be a roofie; I don't know. It doesn't matter what drug it was at this point, but it was strong enough to knock him out.'

'And what? Have her way with him while he was unconscious? That is…' he trailed off.

'Sick? Sure.'

He rubbed his face with his hands. 'Why would she drug you, though? Where do you fit in all of this?

'Oh, she had enough reasons. Out of spite, revenge, to get me out of the way, whichever worked. I didn't know what hit me after I had that glass of wine. I was lucky I went to the room.'

'And where did Jan go?'

'I don't think it affected him right away, but when we left the bar, we ran into Lloyd.'

'And what, Jan went into the room with Lloyd and Sasha for a threesome on their wedding night? That's wild.'

I dropped my head to the floor. 'He wasn't with Sasha.'

'What?'

'Lloyd wasn't with Sasha. He was with someone else.'

'What do you mean he was with someone else?' he asked, confused.

'He was with that model, the influencer… Yovanna.'

Lucien stared at me, his mouth in a perfect 'O' shape.

'Let's not jump to the wrong conclusions. There could be many reasons why she was with him,' he said.

'Really? How many reasons could there be? It was his wedding night, and he fell to his death a few hours later. Lloyd seemed startled that Jan was there, and he left the hotel, and Jan went after him. Cassie could have been in her room watching from the window or somewhere nearby.'

'Does Sasha know about any of this?'

'I don't know, but my guess is no.'

'And have you told this to the police?'

'Not yet.'

He stood and paced around the kitchen.

'When I went after them,' I continued, 'Apolonia came out of nowhere and gave me a shove.'

'Apolonia? What the fuck?'

'I haven't established why Apolonia was there, not yet, at least. But she pushed me and went after them.'

'So, you think Jan confronted Lloyd, Apolonia and Yovanna, and they must have gone back to the wedding, pretended everything was fine and then what? What happened to Jan?'

'Maybe he felt off, and Cassie found them and told Lloyd, Apolonia and Yovanna to return to the party, and she stayed with Jan.'

'And what? Had sex with him while he was out of it?' Lucien asked.

'I don't know.'

'Did you tell him any of this?'

'Not yet. I don't know how to break it to him. All of this is based on what I think.'

'But Cassie drugged you, Emily.'

'Yes. And there is something else...' I said.

He waited.

'After the wedding, I found a note that said it hoped I had fun at the wedding with a condom attached to it. Jan got a thong.'

'And you think Cassie sent those?'

'I'm not sure, but that's what I suspect.'

He sighed. 'I'll fucking kill her. I will kill her going after you and Jan like that. It's disgusting. I'm sick and tired of watching people I care about getting hurt.'

'Lucien, please don't talk like that.'

He clutched his hands into fists. 'That is assault!'

The ugly word roamed around us like that stench that wouldn't go away. But no matter how much we avoided it and tried to find synonyms for it, that was what it was.

'We don't know if it is. We have no proof, and if we are going to the police, we need proof, or else they won't take us seriously,' I reasoned.

'This is a private matter, Emily. No need to involve the police. I'm sick of the police.'

'Spiking people's drinks without them knowing is a crime. If it is an assault, she could go to prison.'

'I have to speak to Jan,' he said. 'He hasn't regained his memory yet, I presume.'

'He is hosting a gathering at his apartment. Do you know about that?'

'Yes, I've seen it, but I wasn't planning to go, but now I have to.'

'Better if you don't. Let me go. Yovanna is going to be there. I have to ask her a few things.'

'Like what? You think she will admit she was having an affair with Lloyd?'

'We don't know if she was having an affair with Lloyd. Maybe Sasha knew about it.'

He pulled a face. 'Sasha knows nothing about this.'

'How do you know?'

'Because I know her.'

'Did you take photographs at the wedding?'

'A few, yes. Why?'

'Can I see them?'

'I already showed them to the police.'

'Just show them to me.'

He took out his phone from his pocket, tapped on the screen, and handed me his phone. I flipped through the selfies of Lucien with the guests. There were a few of Sasha and Lloyd at the venue. Someone must have taken a photo of Lucien with a woman with black hair who had lots of make-up and had her hands placed on her stomach. I flipped the photo, then went back and zoomed in. The photo was taken near the bar, and I scanned it thoroughly. In the background, Anna was talking to a man in a suit and a man with long hair, Lloyd, and beside him was Yovanna.

Chapter Thirty-Five

I went to Jan's apartment earlier than indicated. I could hear music, something soft with an Arabic influence. I knocked on the door, and clutched the bottle of champagne I had bought from the shop down the street. The door opened, and Cassie appeared before me and didn't open the door wider for me to go in. I arranged my face, hoping it hid my surprise.

'Cassie! Hello, how are you?' I said. 'You look lovely.'

She seemed to be taken aback by my upbeat greeting. 'I'm good, thank you. And you?'

'I'm very well,' I said, waving the bottle of champagne. 'I brought supplies.'

She didn't move from the door but stared at me, and her hair was so orange it hurt my eyes. I tried to look over her shoulder but only saw the black and gold folding screen. My stomach clenched, hoping she hadn't drugged him again. But that would be stupid since he had guests coming over.

'Where is the stunning host?' I asked.

'He's—'

'Emily!' Jan called out. 'Is that you?'

He appeared behind Cassie. 'Darling, don't just stand there. Come in.'

Cassie had no choice but to get out of the way so I could go through. I let him give me pecks on the cheek and his cologne, a mix of leather and honey, went straight to my head. He took the champagne bottle from my hand and disappeared into the next room.

'Wine?' he called out.

'Um... sure,' I replied.

Cassie had her hands across her chest, which raised her ample bosom. 'You're early.'

She said this scornfully and made little effort to hide it, fearing I would ruin all of her plans. Again.

'I have to wake up early... For work, so I have to leave early,' I explained.

'Tomorrow is a Saturday. Aren't you in marketing?' she remarked.

'I'm self-employed. If I don't work, I starve. No pay cheque for this one. Jan! Do you need any help?' I called out, locating where he went, leaving Cassie and her scorn behind.

Jan appeared, holding two glasses of wine. There was another knock on the door. That had to be Lucien. The plan was for him to arrive after me to distract Cassie while I filled Jan in on all the details. Lucien and I suspected she would be there early to have some alone time with the object of her affection.

I took the wine glasses from Jan's hand, placed them on a flat surface, and opened the first door I found as I heard Lucien greet Cassie and her with a contemptuous tone saying, 'I didn't know you were coming.'

I shoved Jan inside the room.

'What are you doing?' he asked after I closed the door and locked it.

We were in a bathroom. It was black tiled with a golden feature wall. Two fluffy black towels hung in the towel dryer, and his cologne lingered.

'She is the one who drugged us,' I whispered.

He stared at me. 'What?'

'We left her alone in the bar when we went to the bathroom. It gave her plenty of time.'

'Wait, why would she do that? And how do you know?'

'Lucien told me she has this huge crush on you,' I said, ignoring his questions.

'Oh, that? That was years ago, and now she's hooking up with Lucien.'

'She used Lucien as the spare wrench. She never got over it, the infatuation she has with you.'

He sat down on the toilet. 'Oh, that's bullshit.'

'Is it?'

He thought about this and looked slightly perturbed that it could be true.

'Forgive my bluntness, but did you sleep with her at any point?'

He looked up at me. 'Yeah, a few times.'

I sighed. 'That explains it then.'

'It explains nothing.'

'Did you break it off?'

'There was nothing to break off, we weren't in a relationship, and we're adults. She understood what it was.'

'Did she? I don't think she understood the terms and conditions.'

'There was nothing to understand. I showed up, we had sex, and I left. Simple.'

'Sweetheart, it might have been for you, but not for her. She wanted more.'

He rubbed his face with his hands. 'What are you saying, Emily? Did anything come to you about that night? Something must have come to you for you to be telling me all of this. Just tell me what you know.'

I knelt on the floor before him and told him everything, all that came to me, and after I finished, Jan buried his face in his hands.

'This is the most fucked up, messed up thing I have ever heard!' he cried.

'This is a lot to take in,' I said. 'She must have sent you the thong and the note to me.'

He gaped at me, his jaw hanging open.

'Who else would do that if not her? It was like she was sending us a message that she knew.'

He got up abruptly, and I grew alarmed. Standing, he was six feet two. I stood an entire foot shorter than him. Stopping him would be a challenge, if not impossible. I placed my hand on his to stop him from doing something rash.

'Act like you normally do.'

'She might be suspicious already. Me and you being locked in here.'

'Lucien is with her. He's keeping her occupied with his excuses.'

Jan's face lit up upon hearing Lucien's name. 'He's here?'

'Yes.'

'I know you're angry, but please do not let her know we're onto her.'

He glanced back at me. 'I'm not angry. I'm fucking livid. I remembered who went into Lloyd's room.'

'You do?'

'Yes.'

'When did it come to you?'

'A few days ago, it was quite a shock.'

'Well, tell me, who was it?' I asked.

He opened the bathroom door. 'You'll find out soon enough.'

#

The guests were Sasha, Cassie, Lucien and me. We gathered in his living room and made small talk, but the air was thick around us. Jan sat far away from Cassie on the armchair while Cassie, Sasha and Lucien took the sofa. I remained on my feet by leaning against the window. At one point, Sasha stood and disappeared somewhere. I placed my glass on the coffee table and followed her while the others talked about a festival they went to a few years back. Yovanna had made no appearance yet, and I was growing anxious that she might not come.

I found Sasha lingering in the kitchen, wiping her nose with a kitchen towel.

'Oh,' she said. 'Sorry.'

'No need to apologise. Are you all right?'

'I miss him. It's so hard. Will it ever go away?'

I wanted to tell her it would, but I didn't want to lie to her. 'It will get better in time, but focus on yourself. It's all right to think about it once in a while. To think of him and miss him.'

'Do you miss him? Your ex. Ed was his name, right?'

I thought about this. Of the four years I'd spent with him, and when I was faced with a stranger who hit me in my home because I refused to take him back.

'I think of him, yes, but our breakup wasn't...' I trailed off. 'Civil.'

'Did he hurt you?' she asked.

I lowered my head and nodded.

The silence was understood between us.

'Men can be such... wankers,' she said. 'I don't understand how it got to this.'

I rubbed her shoulder and looked her in the eye. Her fake eyelashes were so long that I didn't know how she could see or keep her eyes open.

'Can I tell you something?' I asked her.

She rubbed her nose with the paper towel and nodded. 'Yes, of course.'

'I saw Lloyd and Yovanna going into the hotel together. Did you know about that?'

'Yes, of course, I know about it. They were on their way to collect a few items from our room.'

'I see,' I said. 'Was Lloyd good friends with her?'

'They were friendly, sure. They went to college together.'

I lifted my eyebrow in surprise. 'Why didn't you tell me this before?'

'I'm telling you now. They both studied graphic design. Did you manage to get your memory back from that night? Is that why you're asking me this?'

I nodded.

'Tell me everything. I need to know.'

Why did Lloyd run away from Jan then if it was so innocent? And why was Apolonia there?

Chapter Thirty-Six

Yovanna arrived an hour later and not alone. Apolonia was with her. They both looked beautiful. Apolonia wore a black velvet dress. Yovanna wore a fishnet t-shirt with a bikini top underneath and a short black skirt with a small slit. There were exaggerated greetings and air kisses when they turned to me. Both girls blinked at me. I was the one who did not blend in there. I was dressed in a white blouse and beige trousers, and nude high heels to make up for my petite frame when being in a room of people that glowed.

Apolonia looked confused, and Yovanna turned and pretended I wasn't there.

'It seems you're everywhere nowadays,' Apolonia said. 'Shouldn't you be hanging around with people your own age?'

'Rude,' I said without hesitation.

'Well, it's true. I mean, you're well into your thirties,' she pointed out.

So what? I had seen the pictures of the festivals this lot went to, mixing themselves with people who were well into their fifties, and I should hang around with people my age? I knew what she meant. I didn't belong there. I didn't dye my hair with extravagant colours, have piercings or wear buckets of make-up and fake eyelashes. I wasn't coated in black and wearing boots with thick rubber soles. I wasn't one of them, and I never would be. They always would be in a different league. More accessible, liberal, more beautiful. Younger. I was normal and ordinary.

'So what if I'm in my thirties?' I said to her. 'Age is just a number.'

She breathed into her wine glass. 'True, but...' She leaned closer as if to tell me a secret. 'He's too much for you.'

I furrowed my eyebrows. 'Who is too much for me?'

'Jan, of course. He's a sweetheart, but he'll outgrow you.'

God, she thought Jan and I were a couple.

'Maybe I will outgrow him,' I said.

She laughed. 'No honey, you have no more growing to do.'

Miserable cow!

I moved away from her and lingered in the background, hoping I'd become part of the furniture, but I was curious how this would unfold. I watched them from where I stood by the window. These pretty, glamorous people. On the surface, they looked like a bunch of young people in their twenties just having a conversation, intelligent, opulent and educated, but deep

241

down, it was more complicated. Beneath all that glamour were dysfunctional, reckless people who slept with one another and even shared partners. I wasn't one to judge, but when people were getting attacked, stalked or killed, that was a different story.

Lucien looked at me from across the room, concern clearly readable on his face. This was another reason I held back from allowing him in. We were too different, apart from the bad things that had happened. How could he even find balance? I didn't belong in this lifestyle with these people, with his friends. We were like two different planets. If I hadn't moved in right across the street from where his parents lived, he wouldn't have looked at me, let alone wanted to be with me. Even the first time I saw him was inappropriate, leaning by that wall in an alleyway, his white hair visible under the orange light, the silver pendant that he didn't wear anymore, with a woman between his legs. I should have known right then what I was getting myself into. Now, if things weren't confusing enough, it became more awkward by me sleeping with Jan. I crossed a line that shouldn't have been crossed. I moved across the room and leaned against the wall. They were huddled in a circle. Jan was on the sofa, and Cassie was beside him. The rest sat on cushions on the floor. The air smelled of Jan's strong cologne and incense but of something else, which I couldn't catch, and someone in this room was a killer.

'You want to hear something hilarious?' Jan was saying.

'You always have a hilarious story to tell,' Yovanna said.

'Oh, but this will knock your socks off,' he informed.

Sasha was picking at her nails, deep in thought. Lucien was scrolling on his phone and looked up. Yovanna and Apolonia were waiting for Jan to elaborate, and Cassie drank her wine.

Jan passed a glance at Cassie. 'Why did you do that, darling?'

His voice was low, and the room felt quiet. The music was the only sound in the background.

Cassie looked at him, aghast. 'Do what?'

'It was you,' he said. 'I know it was you. Why did you do that?'

Yovanna and Apolonia stared, utterly shocked. Lucien was looking at Cassie, and so was Sasha.

Cassie smiled nervously. 'I have no idea what you're talking about. Are you being cheeky again?'

'No, I'm not being cheeky. What the fuck, Cassie? It wasn't funny,' Jan said.

Cassie blinked. 'Jesus, what is wrong with you?'

'What is wrong with me? Seriously?' Jan asked, getting angrier. 'If you wanted to have sex, you could have asked. What you did was disgusting.'

'I didn't—'

'I could report you to the police for what you did,' he remarked. 'What did you do to me after I passed out?'

'I've done nothing. It wasn't me,' Cassie said.

'Wait,' Yovanna said. 'What's going on?'

'She drugged Emily and me,' Jan said.

Yovanna gasped.

'It makes sense why you picked a fight,' Lucien weighed in.

'Shut up, you tom cat with three balls,' Cassie hissed.

'Nice,' Lucien said. 'If I'm a tom cat with three balls, what does that make you?'

'I think it's time to leave,' Apolonia said.

'You pushed me,' I said to Apolonia.

Apolonia scowled at me. 'Excuse me?'

'You heard me. You pushed me and kept going. Why did you do that?'

All eyes were on me.

'Ha!' Apolonia spat. 'You were just another drunk bimbo, so sick of this shit. And you were drunk too.' She looked at Jan. 'You guys were out of it. You have no one to blame but yourselves.'

'Sit down!' Jan shouted.

I jumped, and the others gasped in shock. Yovanna and Apolonia glared at him.

'Sit your arses down!' he ordered.

Yovanna and Apolonia looked at each other and then sat down. 'I don't see why you want us here. This is clearly between you folks,' Apolonia said, flipping her blonde hair.

'We're not the ones who drugged you,' Yovanna said.

'No, but I saw you,' he said.

Yovanna and Apolonia exchanged glances.

'Who did you see?' Yovanna asked.

'Not you, her,' he said, pointing his finger at Apolonia.

Apolonia chuckled. 'You saw me? Where?'

'When I returned to the hotel the morning after the wedding. I was still out of it, but I saw you going into Lloyd and Sasha's room.'

Now it was my turn to be surprised. 'What? How did you—'

'Why do you think I hosted this little gathering?' Jan asked.

He took a sip of wine, looking pleased with himself.

'You should have told me,' I said.

'I'm telling you now,' he said.

Sasha glanced at Apolonia. 'It was you!'

Apolonia looked at Sasha. 'He was drunk. He has no idea what he's talking about.'

'I don't know what you did to me.' He passed a disgusted look at Cassie, who looked pale and afraid. 'But I saw you when I returned to my room that morning. I might have been hungover, but I know it was you,' Jan explained, looking directly at Apolonia. 'You thought no one was watching, that the corridor was empty, but it wasn't. It was *you*.'

The silence stretched in the room.

'Why?' Sasha asked.

'He's lying, clearly confused,' Apolonia said.

'Am I confused?' Jan asked. 'Because the police are looking into it.'

Colour drained from Apolonia's pretty face.

'You went to the police?' Lucien asked.

'As soon as I got my bearings, I spoke to the female detective, Alison,' he said.

When did he remember all of this? Why didn't he tell me?

Something shifted in Apolonia, and she lowered her head. 'It was an accident. I didn't mean to push him. We were seeing each other in secret, and I thought he was going to leave you, not marry you.'

Sasha stared at her, her expression unreadable, as something dark and ominous fell in the room.

'Lloyd was seeing you in secret?' Sasha asked in disbelief.

'I went there to confront him. I was upset. He went out on the balcony and told me to leave, that he didn't want to see me again, and I pushed him, but not intending to kill him. He lost balance and fell to the edge... I didn't know what to do, so I panicked and left.'

Silence.

A growling sounded, and Sasha was on Apolonia, knocking Yovanna along with her as Sasha had her hands around Apolonia's neck, calling her obscenities. Cassie sat there, frozen, unable to believe how this came to happen. Jan and Lucien pushed Sasha off Apolonia as I called the police while Apolonia rose to her feet and bolted to the door.

Chapter Thirty-Seven

Apolonia was found and arrested a few blocks away from the apartment. Cassie remained frozen, unable to move, and finally confessed she did drug us and sent the underwear to him and the note to me, but she had done nothing to Jan when he was passed out. She just wanted to punish him for the pain he'd caused her and me because I had taken what was hers. Jan and I could have pressed charges, but we wanted no more drama.

Still, it didn't explain why Lloyd ran away if it was to collect items from the hotel. I guessed we would never find out. Maybe Lloyd did it out of drunkenness.

I had to go to the police station to answer a few questions and for them to take my statement. On my way out of the room, I ran into Ben. He was holding a cup of coffee, looking wary and tired. He looked at me and gave me a friendly wave, and reluctantly I waved back. My phone buzzed in my bag at that moment, and it was a number I did not recognise.

'Hello?' I asked

'Is this Emily Clarke?' a man said. 'It's Stephen, Agnes Parker's son.'

I moved away from the corridor, away from all the commotion, and I stopped dead in my tracks as he delivered the news.

Mrs Parker had passed away.

After I ended the call, I went to the bathroom, found a stall and cried. Cried in a way as if I had lost someone important to me. And Agnes, despite being nosy, was important to me. I cried for her, for Sylvain, Amanda, Ed, Travis, and even for the lives that were destroyed because of this.

I didn't know where Lucien was, probably with the police still answering questions. With red and puffy eyes, I hurried out of the police station. I walked away from everything, especially from them. I wanted it to go away, to be over.

#

The funeral was held in St. Alfege Church in Greenwich, a beautiful medieval church with a tower. Two smart Mercedes were parked out front, and the hearse gleamed under the grey afternoon light, the back windows packed with a rainbow of flowers. I went to the church, where Agnes's son stood by the door wearing a black suit. I shook his hand and gave him my condolences. The church didn't have that many people, and I recognised most of the neighbours, to who I gave polite nods in greeting. Among them was Olivia. The news must have reached her, but to fly back in the middle of her holiday to attend the funeral surprised me, especially since Olivia wasn't friendly with Agnes. Olivia moved to make space, and I sat next to her.

'I thought you were on holiday,' I whispered.

'I flew back to pay my respects.'

'But—'

'My husband stayed behind.'

A casket was on the altar, together with a large photo of Agnes beaming at the camera. There was a polished, flower-topped coffin; it looked rather large. *Such a big casket for a small woman,* I thought. As the last of the mourners filed in, Stephen walked in along with the priest, and the service began. I scanned the church looking for Lucien. I thought he would come and pay his respects, but I didn't see him.

Afterwards, as we stood outside, Olivia put on her sunglasses.

'Have you spoken to Lucien?' I asked her.

'Yes, of course I have. He's staying with me for the time being. You haven't spoken to him?' she asked.

I shook my head. 'Not yet. I thought he would come to the funeral.'

'He's visiting Henry today,' she informed.

'Ah,' I said. 'Well, I'd better be going.'

'If you want to speak to him, you can come over,' she said.

'No, it's fine. I'll text him later,' I said.

'Whatever you say, Emily. I would ask you to come over for a cup of coffee, but I have to go to the office. There are a few things I have to go over. Are you going to be okay?'

Would I be okay? With lots of therapy, I might be.

#

Jan had been in touch to check on me and give me a few updates. Sasha had moved back in with her parents in Dorset until she figured out her next move. He was no longer friends with Cassie and said he'd be crazy if he remained friends with her. How could he trust her after what she had done? He also told me he planned to take a break from modelling and resume his travels. He traded his car with a camper van, following his father's footsteps, and was going where fate led him. He told me to text him if I'd like to join him, and for a moment, I was tempted. Just to leave it all behind and explore. But of course, I wasn't going to join him. I wondered if he texted Anna and told her the same thing. It didn't matter. Anna had moved on and met a lawyer, and their relationship seemed promising.

I shut my laptop, made a sandwich for dinner, and ate it in front of Netflix. When the buzzer sounded, I was fighting the urge not to rush down to the store and buy a bottle of wine. I wasn't expecting anyone, so I paused the movie and went to see who it was. I stared at the screen as I pushed the button and opened the door, waiting with my hands across my chest. I heard the lift open, then footsteps and Lucien appeared dressed in a black hoodie and black jeans torn on the kneecaps. His platinum blonde hair floated over his waist. There were dark circles under his eyes from lack of sleep or stress.

'I'll be quick,' he said.

There was a certain urgency in him, as if he were in a hurry. I offered for him to come in, but he refused.

'If I had to leave tonight, would you come with me?' he asked.

'What?'

'If I had to leave tonight to live in Edinburgh, would you come with me?' he repeated.

'Um…'

It sounded crazy and unplanned. I couldn't leave. What about my life here in London? But what sort of life was it, really? I used to have a life here, but now? Could I do it?

Could I take this big leap for this guy who claimed he loved me? I crossed my hands under my chest and considered this, weighing my options. Work wasn't a problem. I could do it anywhere, and Edinburgh wasn't that far. Some would say that this was so romantic, to have a man who loved you asking you to go away with him, but I wasn't sure. Could I trust him? Could I leave it all behind and be with him?

'Yes or no, Emily?' Lucien said impatiently.

Chapter Thirty-Eight

One year later…

The tram rumbled past as I walked my way to Princes Street. The air was crisp, and I wrapped my scarf around my neck and hurried my pace. I turned the corner up to a long hill, took the keys from my pocket, and opened the door to the cottage where Lucien and I had been living together for the past year.

'I'm home,' I announced. 'You wouldn't believe the meeting I had. Gosh, so bonkers. I need a new career.'

I took off my boots, my scarf, and then my coat. 'Where are you, you silly sausage?'

No response.

Was he supposed to go out today? I was sure he said he was going to be home all day. Maybe he had to head to London to see his parents. Was it Henry's or Amelia's day? No, today was Friday. I located the kitchen. It was empty.

'Peanut!' I called out.

Nothing.

I placed my bag on the kitchen table and rummaged through it to find my phone. There was a text, but it was from Anna, nothing from him. I placed the phone down on the table and put the kettle on. I left the kitchen and padded to the bedroom. He wasn't there either. Maybe he went to run errands or had a dose of inspiration and went to take photographs. He had his own studio two doors down from the cottage. He still modelled sometimes, but not as much.

After he came to my apartment with his insane proposal, he urged me to pack a bag, leave everything else behind, and worry about the rest later. It was the craziest thing I had ever done. He had the car ready, and he was going to drive us there. It would be an adventure, he said. He planned to get to Edinburgh by the morning. As he drove and I looked at the passing street, I almost told him to stop the car and take me back. What was I doing? What about my parents? What about Anna? I couldn't leave. It was insane. Where were we going to live?

'Lucien, what are we doing?' I asked.

'Moving on,' he said.

'Why Edinburgh?'

He looked at me. 'Why not Edinburgh?'

'Well, it is a very beautiful city.'

'It is, and it's far as one can get, but still in Britain,' he said.

'I thought you would go to Berlin.'

'Why would I do that?'

'Just a guess,' I said.

My parents were baffled, of course, moving away with the guy who had brought so much chaos into my life. To move that far without them ever meeting him? They met, of course, after we had settled and he found this cottage. He had lots of money saved up since he'd sold the house in Greenwich and Exeter and had spare cash from his modelling days.

At first, I felt weird about having a man buying a house, and I didn't have to spend a cent, but as time passed, the feeling went away, and now one year after the things we went through, we had found balance and something that resembled peace.

I moved around the elegant rooms. Everything had been decorated by him in colours of purple, silver and black. He found the most beautiful things from antique and charity shops. I changed into something more comfortable: sweatpants and a tatty sweater, and returned to the kitchen where the kettle had boiled. I made a cup of tea and took it to the laundry room.

Today, it was time for the most tedious task of all. If only there was a way for clothes to magically wash and iron themselves. What a blessing it would be. I put on a playlist on Spotify and sorted out the piles. The blacks were mainly his, and the colourful ones were mine. I started with the blacks, going through the pockets to ensure nothing was there. I filled the washing machine and switched it on. I turned to leave, taking a sip of tea, when I noticed an envelope lying on the floor.

I frowned and picked it up. It was addressed to Lucien, and it was from prison. I placed the mug on the washing machine, staring at the letter. Another letter like the others Henry had sent. Why write a letter when Lucien was visiting him? This must have dropped from one of his pockets, and Lucien must have forgotten about it. The envelope was torn, which meant he'd opened it and read it. With shaking hands, I took it out and unfolded the letters.

Dear Lucien,

I don't know if you read any of the letters I sent you, so this is another attempt to speak to you. I hope you read this and get in touch. It would be nice to see you. I know this wasn't easy for you, and I'd be pushing it to ask for your forgiveness. I know your mum hasn't made things easier; she has done awful things. As I said in the other letters, Emily had been here to speak to me. I admit seeing her had thrown me off. She was the last person I expected would come and see me, especially when she mistook her speaking to you as a threat rather than a warning from your mother. And my approach was hostile, and I wasn't very nice to her, but she came either way.

Anyway, I'm sure Emily has told you all of this, and she is very fond of you, Lucien. I'm still waiting for you to come and see me, so we can talk properly. You owe me that, at least.

Yes, I was angry when you visited and told you I didn't want to speak to you again, but I am just a grumpy old man. I was never known for my patience, and I treated you appallingly when you were a child, given what your mother did. Taking it out on you was wrong. But you did wrong, Lucien, and you know I sacrificed everything for you. Don't you dare tell me I don't love you. Would a father who never loved a child cover for him like this? So, you can have your life, your freedom? You pushed Sylvain down that well; you killed my son, and it drove your mother to utter despair, and she never recovered from it, so much so it turned her into a monster. I'm not saying you turned her that way, but you were partly responsible. That was the main issue with you. You never take responsibility for your actions. Yes, it was an accident, and you didn't mean it. We had to live with the guilt to protect you for the rest of our lives, and you pushed him for what? Because you didn't want him to go out with a girl you had a crush on? Did he deserve that? We had to keep him down there and pretend that he was missing, then lie all over again that I pushed my son instead of you. Very selfish, Lucien, but you always have been. You disobeyed your mother and me even when we told you never to go to that house again. But the guilt made you do that, didn't it?

So, boy. You have your cross to bear, as it seems you had forgotten.

Reply to this letter or come to see me. Do what you will, but I will continue to send these to Olivia until you finally cave in. Maybe one day she will open one of these damn letters and see you for who you truly are.

Your father,

Henry.

A stabbing pain of the past came hard and strong, making it very real. The past was pressing down on me, suffocating me. What had I just read? No, it was a lie. Henry was lying. *No. No. No.* This couldn't be true, could it? I knocked the mug, and it smashed on the floor, and liquid splashed all over my legs. Was it true? But how could it be true?

I lay my body against the washing machine as something came to me, something Travis had said. *Do you honestly believe she turned out that way just because of what happened with his brother? Do you? The experience didn't help, but he didn't make life easy for her.*

That she was Amelia.

Then at once, Ben's words came to me, hard and strong, knocking me over. *Something is off about that guy. I can't put my finger on what.*

Oh my God.

Lucien had said he had the flu that night. Amelia confirmed this, and Henry said this too, if I wasn't mistaken. Sylvain went into the room and told Lucien that he had pulled a neat one. Then, he left again, where Sylvain had to face his father's wrath. They were down by the well, and Henry accidentally pushed Sylvain down the well.

But what I had was a confession from his parents. They kept their promise till the very end to protect Lucien. It was the other way around; Lucien might have been sick, couldn't go out with his brother and had no choice but to stay in bed while Sylvain went out. He came back later and told Lucien he had hooked up with Julie. Lucien got angry. There must have been an argument that led the two teenage boys to the back garden where the well was, and Lucien pushed Sylvain down the well. His parents had two choices: call the authorities and Lucien would be sent to a juvenile prison and bear a criminal record for the rest of his life, and Henry's reputation in the army would be ruined. Amelia thought of an immediate plan. They reported Sylvain as missing and instructed Lucien on what to say.

They moved out of that house, hoping to never return. Lucien, however, couldn't let it go and went to the house in Exeter without his parents' knowledge on the anniversary of his brother's death. Out of guilt, I suppose, but to take me over there? I remembered when I looked down at the well to see nothing but pitch black, and when I turned, I found Lucien standing there right behind me. I asked myself if he would push me. I think he was afraid I might have sensed something. He went there to check that everything was in order. However, he had no idea there were two more bodies down there. Amanda's and Ed's.

This experience had shaken both of his parents. Amelia was already unhinged, and her beloved son pushing his brother down that well made her worse.

Henry wanted to control some sense of order and get on with their lives to move past it and, in return, gain sympathy from people.

No matter how much Henry tried to maintain Lucien, Lucien had other ideas which would piss off his orderly, narrowed-minded father. It all made sense. Amelia had said that Henry was afraid of Lucien. He let Lucien do whatever he wanted when he grew older, grow his hair long, become a model, sleep around, and leave the house whenever he saw fit. Henry could not control him and Amelia well… Lucien was her favourite son, and Henry would have done the right thing and said it was an accident, but Amelia would not have it. Henry's life might have been a living hell after that accident, and he couldn't do anything about it. He had a son who wasn't his and an unstable wife. Henry confessed he had pushed Sylvain down the well because he preferred being in prison rather than waking up and facing hell every day.

I always found it odd that Lucien had slept with Julie when she had been questioned by the police in connection with the disappearance of his missing brother. Why would anyone do that? It seemed strange to me, and he was so nonchalant about the whole thing. It made sense because he wanted Julie even after years had passed. Because he knew she had nothing to do with Sylvain's disappearance.

A sound came out of me like a wounded animal. The spin dryer rolled into the washing machine, causing it to vibrate as tears smeared down my face. This past year had been bliss. We were happy, and I could only stare in awe at the beautiful creature that Lucien was. True to his word, he turned his life around because he wanted to be with me. He had his career and me, all he devoted his life to. He didn't want children. He found babies annoying and loud and toddlers with their sticky hands touching things. I reasoned that babies and toddlers grow up eventually, stop being annoying, and learn to wash their hands. He was adamant, and he shot me one icy glare and made me realise arguing with him was pointless. So, I made that sacrifice for him, and now this. This was what I got. This was too much.

I thought of the times I watched him when he was invited to an event and how he showed me off, the look of pride on his face. Photographers asking him if they could take his picture, and him obliging. I watched the master at his work. Did he really push his brother? Had Lucien been secretly jealous of his older brother?

If Lucien had never reconnected with Henry, where was he going? Where did he go when he told me he went to London to visit his father? Twice a week, Tuesday for Amelia and Thursday for Henry. He even told this to Olivia and to his friends. He was lying to me and to everyone else. Nobody was going to check if he was visiting Henry. Why would we check? Why would we question him? I thought of Henry's letter pleading with his son to resume their relationship. He was locked up and couldn't do anything about it. He was helpless and had no control over the situation.

I reread the letter twice, three times, four times and then scanned the washroom. The machine had stopped, and it clicked to show it was ready. I could go to the authorities with this. It would change everything. Amelia would remain in prison. She had killed two people, but Henry? They covered up the accident and made people believe their son was missing.

I thought of the times I looked at that face, into those innocent green eyes. Was there any hint? Had I been so captivated by Lucien that I failed to see it? What I saw was a somewhat tragic, flawed, but very beautiful young man.

I considered what I should do. I could confront him about it and destroy everything. Maybe I should buy a camper van and go explore. Run away and not tell anyone, but I couldn't do that.

I placed the letter on the surface of the washing machine, took a photo of the two pages, then left the washroom and emerged into the hall, where the coat hanger stood by the front door. Lucien's custom-made coats hung there, and I folded the letter and slipped it inside the damask coat pocket that carried his sweet scent.

The only logical thing to do was pretend I never saw that letter and had never read it. It happened over a decade ago; it didn't matter. It wouldn't change anything and would certainly not bring his brother back. Lucien would go to prison for the rest of his life. His parents had worked hard to protect this secret, and I would do the same. They had made their choice when it happened, and I wasn't going to correct it, and I had seen enough pain. No need to stir things up again when there was calm. Lucien had learned from his mistakes. On Thursdays, he might have gone to take photographs in London instead of seeing Henry. I intervened by trying to reunite Lucien with Henry, and Lucien had his reasons why he didn't want to speak to his father anymore. I did what I had to do by trying to do the right thing. Why didn't he tell me, though? Why tell me he was visiting him in prison? Why lie about it? Was that why he had been so angry at me after he was released from the hospital, and I mistook his coldness for rejecting him when it had nothing to do with that? It was because I had the audacity to go to prison to speak to Henry.

I put the kettle on again, reached for the paper towels, and returned to the washroom. I picked up the broken mug, wiped the liquid off the floor and mopped it, hiding all evidence of this shocking revelation. I put the clothes in the dryer and watched them roll for a minute or two before putting the coloured clothes in the washing machine. Just a woman doing the everyday chores that were required. When that was done, I threw the broken mug and kitchen towels in the bin and turned to make another fresh mug of tea.

I heard the key in the front door, the door open and close, and my heart stopped.

'Oi!' Lucien called out.

'In the… kitchen.' My voice broke, and I cleared my throat.

I listened to the sound of heavy boots, and he walked in glorious as usual, dressed in a black shirt with frills, decorated with jewellery and smelling like a spa. I quickly looked away even though I had arranged my face to neutral, but I was afraid he might catch something.

'Where were you?' I asked.

'I went to run some errands,' he said.

'Tea?' I asked.

'Sure.'

I opened the cupboard, produced his black mug with a white bat, put in a tea bag, and poured hot water. He moved closer to me, his six-foot frame towering over me, and my heart slowed. I kept my eyes low, busying myself with the tea. He leaned closer and planted a kiss on my cheek. I smiled and sniffed, and he took the mug of tea.

'Where do you want to go tonight?' he asked.

'Tonight?' I asked.

'Yeah, it's Friday. Date night…'

'Oh… it doesn't matter. You choose.'

I had my back to him and took a sip of the still-scalding tea.

'Emily!' he called out.

I turned, facing him. He was sitting on the chair, one leg on top of the other.

'Yes, darling?'

'Are you all right?'

'Yes, of course, I had this meeting with demanding clients. You know how it is.'

'Hmm,' he said. 'I shall take my queen somewhere special then.'

He became background noise as I saw a sixteen-year-old boy with long blonde hair shoving his older brother so hard that he fell into the well. Killing him. The hairs on my body stood on end.

'Emily!'

I was snapped back to the present and looked at this beautiful man. His large green eyes penetrated me as if he could see through my soul. That was when I realised he knew, and it was the secret we would keep.

\#

The Secret They Kept: Book 1

Emily Clarke thought her dreams were coming true. Her business was thriving and she was moving into a beautiful new house. Yet this dream quickly morphed into a nightmare.

Rocks being thrown at her windows. Haunting messages written on glass. Items mysteriously disappearing.

Emily's nerves are on edge, which is only made worse by the man across the street constantly screaming at his wife. By befriending their son, Lucien, she learns a dark truth about the street she now calls home. Lucien has a brother who went missing ten years ago, as did the last occupant of Emily's house.

Emily wants to believe these ominous events are past history until her ex-boyfriend vanishes without a trace. Now, she's convinced she is a pawn in someone's twisted game.

Can she uncover who is behind these disappearances before becoming their next victim?

Secrets and Lies: Book 2

Emily Clarke is still haunted by the events that unraveled a year ago.

Not having seen or spoken to Lucien, she is struggling to sell her home in Greenwich while using alcohol to help her cope.
Arriving home from the holiday, Emily finds a single red rose outside her door, is it Lucien trying to send her a message?

Then… the attacks begin.

The people she cares for are being attacked by a malicious culprit. With Lucien picking that moment to reappear, Emily can't help but question his motives. Does he know who is behind the vicious crimes? Together, can they put an end to the rash of violence?

The Secret She Kept

Days before her murder, Anthony's friend Lottie lent him her laptop. Curiosity getting the best of him, he clicks on a file and finds videos recorded by her in the year leading up to her death. Within those recordings, she exposes dark secrets someone will kill to keep hidden, and Lottie's toxic relationship with Anthony's long-time friend, Davian.

When Anthony's childhood friend, Davian, is placed under arrest for the murder, Anthony refuses to believe he could do such a thing, but Lottie was infatuated by Davian. More damning evidence piles up. Anthony wonders if it's possible a man he's known for most of his life has kept a sinister side of himself hidden.

Now, Anthony faces an impossible choice; turn the laptop over to the police and risk being accused of hindering the investigation, or try to solve the case himself. Lottie gave him the computer for a reason. There was something there she wanted him to see. Can he put the pieces of the puzzle together in time to uncover the killer?

In Her Words

While she seems to have it all, Sophie Knight is looking for more. When gorgeous and carefree Michael Frisk walks into her life, he offers the excitement and passion she desires.

Sophie is willing to risk everything she has. After all, she is used to concealing things from her husband—like her alcoholism, her unhappiness. But soon she has more to hide. She wakes up one morning in an alcoholic haze and finds bruises on her body, but has no recollection of what happened to her. Was she raped?

When unsettling notes and mysterious phone calls start, Sophie wonders whom she should turn to. Is Michael the cause of the frightening things happening in her life, or is he the answer to her problems?

Theodore: The Neighbour's Cat

My roommate is a serial killer.

And I have been powerless to stop him because I... am a cat.

Don't get me wrong, Dean has never been cruel to me. He provides me with shelter, toys, and plenty of affection. But I have seen his dark side, his brutal treatment of women, and I can't bear to watch anyone else get hurt.

Jane from next door is attractive for a human, not to mention being incredibly kind. That kindness may get her killed. I've seen how Dean looks at her, I know what he's plotting. In his mind, she's his for the taking. I wasn't able to save the others, but I'm not ready to give up. One way or another, I have to figure out how to communicate to Jane that she's in danger.

Can I find a way to warn her in time? Or will she become just another name on his growing list of victims?

The Rich Man

Her beloved disappeared without a word.

When a web of deceit tightens, can a young woman uncover the truth before she's the next to get ghosted? Elena Gomez's heart aches over her boyfriend's betrayal. But determined to pick up the pieces, she squares her shoulders and struggles to rebuild.

And when a handsome and wealthy widower sweeps into her life, she dares hope he's the answer to her prayers. Blossoming under his devoted attention, Elena soon finds herself falling hard for his magnetic charm.

But when she discovers the odd events surrounding his late wife's death, a series of unnerving coincidences send her pulse racing with dread. And when a ghost from her past returns, she fears she's stepped into a trap that could cost her everything.

Can she escape the darkness closing in, or will she be pulled six feet under?

Lost and Found: Book 1

Despite being polar opposites, Phoebe and Adele's friendship has stretched on for years. One a bubbly blonde, the other raven-haired and studious. They seem to have nothing in common, yet the bond between them is unbreakable.

Or so Phoebe thought.

She never believed Adele would hide anything from her until she sees her sneaking off with her handsome neighbour. Feeling betrayed, Phoebe begins to see cracks in their friendship she never noticed before.

Then, Adele vanishes.

Fearing for Adele's safety, Phoebe searches for clues about her disappearance. However, the deeper she digs, the more she realizes she didn't know Adele as well as she thought. Yet as revelations come to light, one mystery remains. What happened to Adele? And how is her disappearance connected to the stranger next door?

Hide and Seek: Book 2

Hope is waning with Phoebe no closer to finding her best friend, Adele. Her suspicions involving her neighbour, Alan, have been cleared, leaving her no other hunches to pursue.

Until the letter arrives.

A message, written in Adele's hand, paints a picture of a side of her friend's life Phoebe never knew. Renewed with the optimism that she is still alive, Phoebe launches back into the investigation. Among the pages of Adele's communications, Phoebe finds evidence pointing to an unlikely suspect...

And yet another connection to Alan.

He seemed so concerned about the investigation, wanting to help in any way he could. Was the man next door a genuine ally? Or working to protect the real culprit?

Till Death Do Us Part.

Abigail thought she achieved the ultimate fairy tale. Handsome movie star meets small-island hotel employee and sweeps her away to his glorious Hollywood mansion. Everything about Carson Levin seems too good to be true... until she steps inside his home.

Every inch of it is just as his sex symbol wife, Taira Anderson, left it before her fatal car accident. But the oddities don't end there.

A presence wanders the halls.
High heels clicking over the floor.
Mysterious splashes in the pool.
The bath filling with water without a soul in sight.

Something or someone is trying to send Abigail a message. But is it a warning... or a threat?

Scan the code to purchase.

Note from The Author

If you enjoy what I write, you can help this little writer out by writing a review on Amazon or Goodreads or any platform of your choice. Reviews are the lifeline for authors and readers trust other readers. If you use social media, spread the word. It will be wonderful to have my book listed with others you have enjoyed.

Love,
J.S Ellis xx

You can sign up for my newsletter and keep updated with new releases, offers, updates and giveaways.

https://joannewritesbooks.com

About the author.

J.S Ellis is a thriller author. She lives in Malta with her husband and their cats, Eloise and Theo. When she's not writing or reading, she's either cooking, eating cheese and chocolate, or listening to good music and enjoying a glass of wine or two.

Website https://joannewritesbooks.com
Facebook https://www.facebook.com/authorJ.SEllis/
Instagram @ author_j.sellis
Goodreads http://bit.ly/2P8a9xx
Pinterest: https://bit.ly/3iqBvrU
Amazon: https://amzn.to/30rbKSq
Bingebooks: https://bingebooks.com/author/j-s-ellis
Bookbub: https://www.bookbub.com/authors/j-s-ellis

Made in the USA
Las Vegas, NV
14 February 2023

67452564R00163